THE EXTRAORDINARY ADVENTURES OF

ORDINARY BOY

BOOK ONE
THE HERO REVEALED

WILLIAM BONIFACE

ILLUSTRATIONS BY STEPHEN GILPIN

HarperCollins*Publishers*

For information address HarperCollins Children's Books, a division of
HarperCollins Publishers, 1350 Avenue of the Americas, New York, NY 10019.
www.harperchildrens.com

Library of Congress Cataloging-in-Publication Data
Boniface, William.
    The hero revealed / by William Boniface ; illustrations by Stephen
Gilpin.— 1st ed.
        p. cm. — (The extraordinary adventures of Ordinary Boy ; bk. 1)
    Summary: Ordinary Boy, the only resident of Superopolis without a
superpower, uncovers and foils a sinister plot to destroy the town.
    ISBN-10: 0-06-077464-9 (trade bdg.)
    ISBN-13: 978-0-06-077464-6 (trade bdg.)
    ISBN-10: 0-06-077465-7 (lib. bdg.)
    ISBN-13: 978-0-06-077465-3 (lib. bdg.)
    [1. Heroes—Fiction. 2. Collectors and collecting—Fiction.] I. Gilpin, Stephen,
ill. II. Title III. Series: Boniface, William. Extraordinary adventures of Ordinary
Boy ; bk. 1.
PZ7.B6416He 2006   2005018676
[Fic]—dc22   CIP
                                                                         AC

Typography by R. Hult
1 2 3 4 5 6 7 8 9 10
❖
First Edition

For Chris Anderson,
To add to your collection.

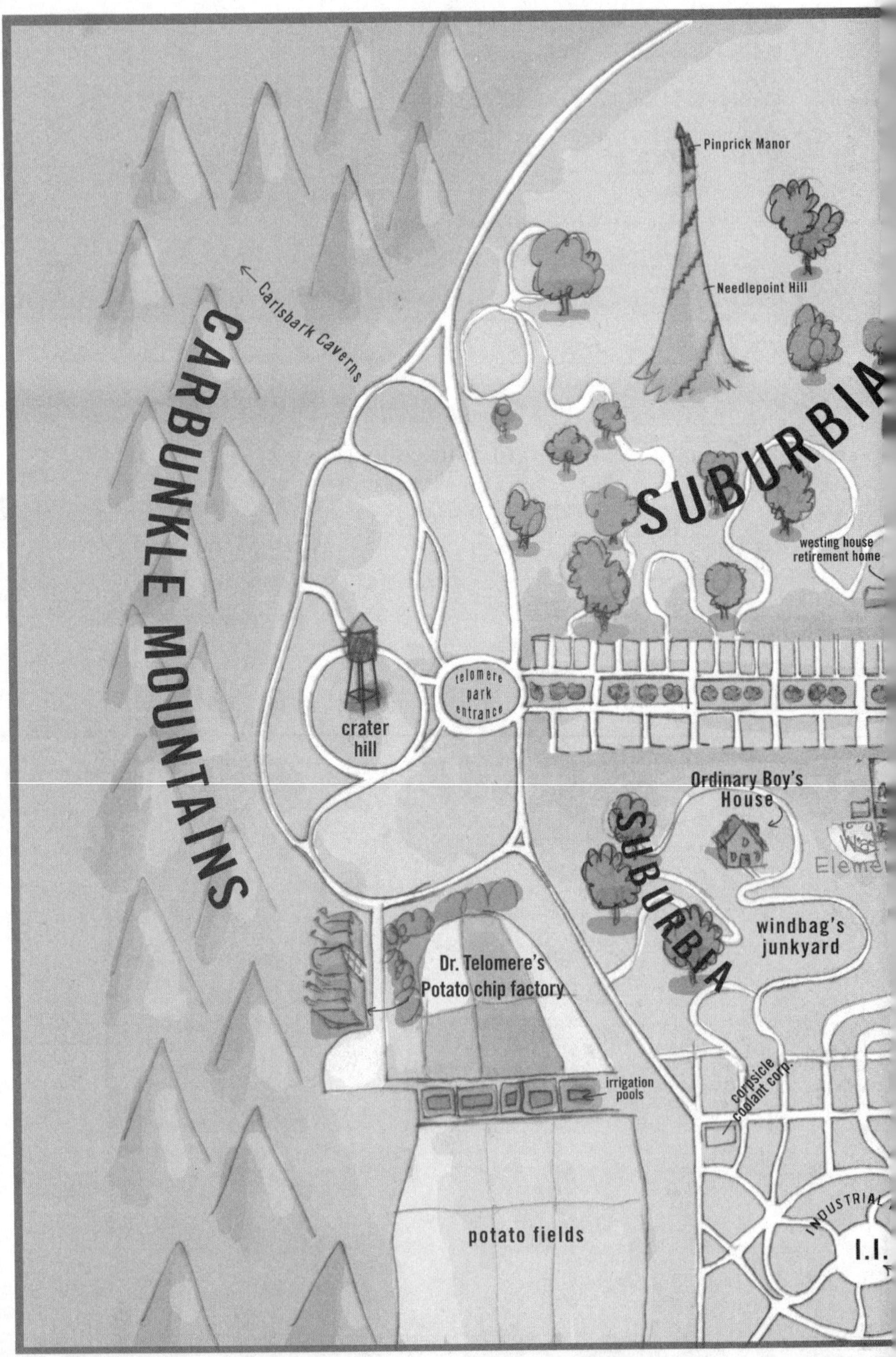

Pinprick Manor
Needlepoint Hill
Carlsbark Caverns
CARBUNKLE MOUNTAINS
SUBURBIA
westing house retirement home
telomere park entrance
crater hill
Ordinary Boy's House
SUBURBIA
windbag's junkyard
Dr. Telomere's Potato chip factory
irrigation pools
corpsicle coolant corp.
potato fields

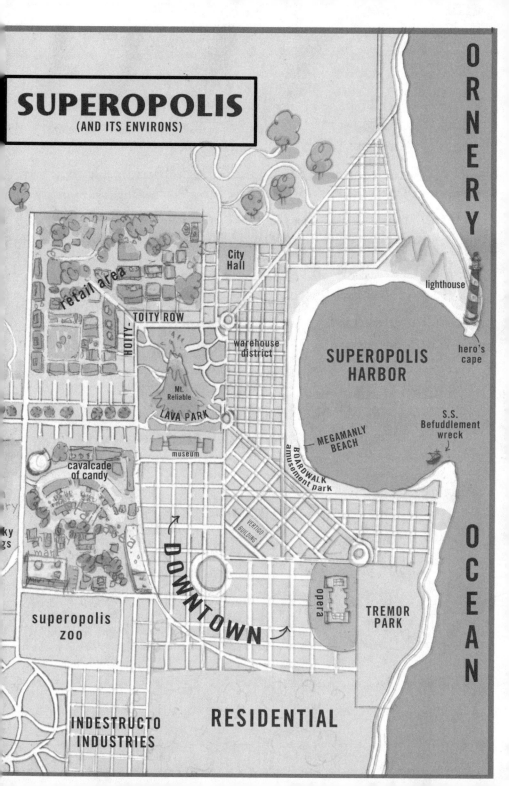

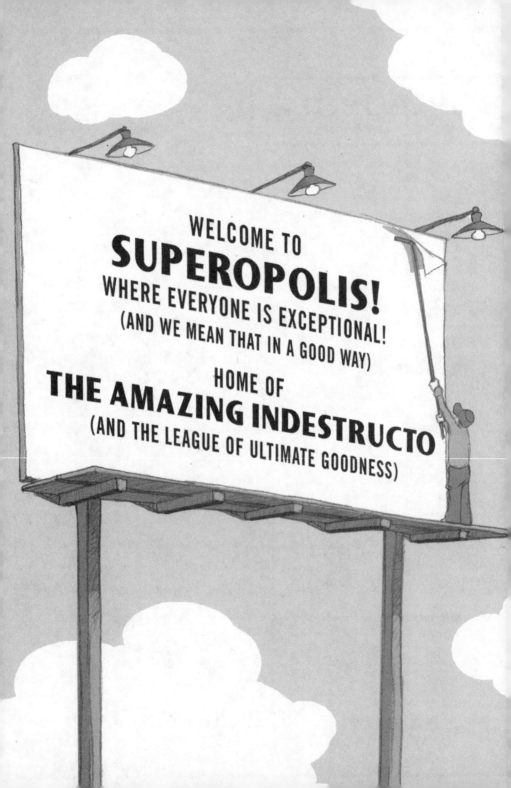

The Astoundingly Unbelievable Secret Origin of Ordinary Boy

Sure, it sounds like a great opening title, but the reality is, well . . . I'm ordinary. I know you're thinking, "What's the big deal? So are most people. That's why it's called being ordinary." The problem is, I live in a place where absolutely no one is ordinary. It's called Superopolis, and, as you might guess with a name like that, this is a city where everyone has some sort of superpower.

Nobody knows why everyone here has a power.

Maybe it's something in the water. Or maybe there's a radioactive meteor buried under the city. Everyone here also eats a lot of potato chips, but I doubt that has anything to do with it. Whatever the cause, it clearly has no effect on me.

You're probably wondering by now what my real name is. Well, I'm wondering, too. You see, in Superopolis, everyone's name has something to do with his or her superpower. It doesn't take too long before a baby starts showing some sort of power—like being able to float, for instance. Then the parents will probably start calling him Floating Baby. They may come up with something a little more original if they happen to be clever—but, frankly, most people aren't. Then, when he gets older, he'll become Floating Boy, and as an adult he'll be known as Floating Man. Get it? That's what happened to me. My parents waited around a long time to give me a name, but all they could say about me was "He's so ordinary." So it stuck, and Ordinary Boy I am.

This is my entry in the *Li'l Hero's Handbook*. Inspiring, isn't it? In spite of what it says about me (which I have to admit is basically correct), the handbook is really pretty fantastic. It gives all sorts of handy information on the people, places, and things of Superopolis. I carry it with me constantly.

NAME: Ordinary Boy. **POWER:** None. **LIMITATIONS:** Where do we begin? **CAREER:** Currently enrolled in Watson Elementary; member of the Junior Leaguers. **CLASSIFICATION:** Unique among Superopolitans, Ordinary Boy's lack of any power earns him our sympathy.

As the handbook makes abundantly clear, everyone here, except for me, has a superpower. The thing is, though, they only have *one* power. You won't find some guy who can fly *and* has X-ray vision *and* is strong enough to lift a truck. It just doesn't work that way. It's one power and one power only. Sadly, just as with looks, talent, and brains, the powers that people end up with are hardly equal.

Some folks have an awesome power, like the Amazing Indestructo, who can't be harmed by anything. And I mean *anything*! There isn't even some goofy, arbitrary substance—like, say, cottage cheese—that he's vulnerable to. He's the leader of Superopolis's most popular group of superheroes, the League of Ultimate Goodness. We never hear much about the other members because the Amazing Indestructo gets all the attention.

On the other hand, there are plenty of people who have powers that are less impressive, like this kid in my class named Puddle Boy. He can create puddles wherever he wants, but who cares? And, to be honest, I'm not entirely certain what those puddles are even made of. Ick! Some things are better left unknown.

Most powers fall somewhere in between, like the Green Thumb, who can make plants grow instantly and owns a successful landscaping business here in

NAME: Amazing Indestructo, The. **POWER:** Invulnerable to all harm. **LIMITATIONS:** None. Oh, to be so perfect! **CAREER:** Leader of the League of Ultimate Goodness for nearly twenty-five years. **CLASSIFICATION:** Superopolis's greatest hero.[*]

[*]SELF-PROCLAIMED.

Superopolis. Even the folks with lesser powers usually find some way to make a living off it. After all, not everyone can grow up to become a crime-fighting superhero—although, of course, that's what every kid in Superopolis wants to be.

As babies, our silk diapers double as our first costumes. By the time we're walking we've begun wearing tights; and once we reach school age, accessories like capes, belts, and masks have become part of every kid's wardrobe. Even the people who don't go on to careers as crime fighters still wear a costume of some kind. Except for me. Since I don't have any kind of power at all, I usually just wear jeans and a T-shirt.

As it says in my profile, I'm part of a team called the Junior Leaguers. It includes Halogen Boy, who glows brighter depending on the amount of apple juice he's been drinking; Tadpole, who can stick his tongue out as far as twenty feet; Plasma Girl, who can turn herself into this goopy jelly-like substance—and then there's Stench. Everything about this guy is strong, especially . . . well, I'll bet you can gas—uh, I mean guess from his name.

I'd like to say that we're always out battling the forces of evil, but the truth is we spend most of our time hanging around our secret headquarters, eating potato chips and reading the latest comic book adventures of the Amazing Indestructo. Despite the fact that

I'm ordinary, they still treat me like a full member of the team.

I'm not sure why I'm so ordinary. Both of my parents have superpowers. My dad, Thermo, is able to make his hands incredibly hot. It may not sound like much of a power, but he can do some amazing things. Lately, he's been trying to become a member of the League of Ultimate Goodness, but he keeps getting turned down. I don't know why. He'd be more useful than most of the current members.

My mom's power is even cooler. And I mean that literally. She can freeze anything just by staring at it really hard. Her name is Snowflake. Sometimes I wonder if their powers canceled each other out when they had me.

Of course, when they were younger, my parents spent most of their time fighting crime. After all, that's what people with superpowers do—at least until they realize they have to get real jobs. Just like any town, ours has some people who aren't very nice. Only here, those people have superpowers, too, which I guess makes them supervillains. It makes sense. You can't really be a superhero if you don't have any villains to battle.

The worst of them is a guy named Professor Brain-Drain. Like his name implies, he can boost his own brain power by draining the intelligence of others. In

Superopolis, this can be a big problem since a lot of people here don't exactly have an excess of smarts to begin with. After all, who needs brains when you have a superpower? Professor Brain-Drain uses his super-smarts to devise all sorts of devious schemes. Luckily, the Amazing Indestructo never fails to foil his plans, which is just one of the reasons he's hands down my number one all-time favorite hero.

SUPEROPOLIS

The City of Heroes! Superopolis is bordered on the east by the Ornery Ocean and on the west by the impassable Carbunkle Mountains. The exact date that the city was settled is unknown, due in large measure to a complete lack of curiosity on the part of Superopolis's citizens. Current residents consider it the perfect place to live and raise families—despite alarmingly frequent volcanic and seismic activity in the area. For an overall view of the city and its environs, please consult the map at the beginning of this book.

CHAPTER ONE

The Cavities of Doom

The Amazing Indestructo sniffed the air as if he could actually smell the odor of evil wafting through the skies of Superopolis. His head tilted one way—and paused—and then the other, revealing both of his perfect profiles. Then the rocket pack on his back burst into life, and he shot into the air like a pillar of fire.

He was only airborne for a matter of seconds before he spotted his quarry. The Brain-Drain Blimp! It looked almost peaceful as it hovered silently above the rooftops of Superopolis's warehouse district. But the Amazing Indestructo wasn't fooled by its pleasingly puffy shape. He knew evil lurked on board. And sure enough, as he watched, the blimp landed and Professor Brain-Drain's minions began unloading hundreds of cases of pilfered property. The Amazing Indestructo spoke into his wrist walkie-talkie.

"Attention, members of the League of Ultimate Goodness," he announced. "I have discovered where Brain-Drain is hiding the stolen tubes of McCavity's Ultra-Paste Tooth Whitener. I'm going in after him."

He turned and looked right into the camera as he said this and flashed his own perfectly white teeth. A moment later, the scene cut to a commercial.

Wow! I thought to myself. *What I wouldn't give to be soaring through the air with Superopolis's greatest hero.* Instead, I had to settle for sitting on the couch on a Saturday morning in my Amazing Indestructo pajamas, watching *The Amazing Adventures of the Amazing Indestructo (and the League of Ultimate Goodness).* And, no, there isn't anything wrong with my typing. That's about the size of the credit that the rest of the league usually gets.

This morning's episode was a new one. In it, AI (that's what we real fans call him for short) was trying to save Superopolis from his greatest enemy, Professor Brain-Drain, who had stolen the city's entire supply of toothpaste.

Brain-Drain is always trying to either take over or destroy Superopolis. He seems to change his mind from week to week as to which one he would rather do. In this week's episode the Professor had so far succeeded

11

with his plan, and everyone's teeth had started to rot away. Everyone's except the Amazing Indestructo's, of course!

As in most episodes, the other members of the League of Ultimate Goodness were helpless (this time because of loose teeth and really bad breath). There are currently ten of them, but usually only five appear in an episode. They always try to help and as the show returned, that's exactly what they were doing.

"The Amazing Indestructo needs us," announced the Crimson Creampuff. "We have to hurry to his aid."

"Whoo-wee! Shurin' if yer breath ain't enough to bring down a whole heap o' bad guys," said Whistlin' Dixie. "And ma two front choppers are wigglin' so fierce I ken barely whistle in tune. I say we go help round up the varmint what done this!"

"Why bother?" groaned Major Bummer. "We've all got to go sometime. It might as well be from halitosis."

This was pretty typical of Major Bummer. He was always depressed and gloomy. I suppose that's how he got his name—although it might also have something to do with his really big butt.

"I could try tunneling my way there," proposed the Moleman, "except my molars are killing me."

"I can immobilize the Professor with my coils of spaghetti," proclaimed Spaghetti Man. The truth is, a ninety-year-old grandmother could break out of the limp noodles he produces from his fingertips.

"That's the attitude, leaguers," said the Crimson Creampuff as he slammed a fist into his hand and then winced in pain. "The Amazing Indestructo needs us and it's time for us to come to his aid!"

Meanwhile, AI had decided to storm Professor Brain-Drain's secret hideout single-handedly. Without hesitation he zoomed straight to the top of the building where the Brain-Drain Blimp was tethered. He crashed through the roof and came face-to-face with his greatest enemy.

"You fiend," he said, as he stood amidst the smoke and dust. "Your plot to deny the people of Superopolis the whitening advantage of McCavity's Ultra-Paste Tooth Whitener is at an end."

And there, standing calmly amid thousands of cases of McCavity's toothpaste, was that supervillain of all supervillains, Professor Brain-Drain—or at least the actor who played him. All the other characters on the show play themselves, but Professor Brain-Drain is always an actor. The funny thing is it never seems to be the same actor. Last week's Brain-Drain had a high-pitched voice. The one before that actually had some hair. This newest one, I noticed, had a big mole on his nose.

I grabbed my copy of the *Li'l Hero's Handbook* and quickly flipped to the entry on Professor Brain-Drain.

The picture was of a man significantly older than the guy on TV, and there was definitely no mole on his nose. Well, if he's retired, I guess it made sense that he doesn't play himself. Of course, his tendency to drain people's intelligence and be superevil may have been a factor as well. I set the handbook back down just as the actor playing the Professor began to speak.

"Ah, the Amazing Indestructo." The egghead of evil chortled. (This was the first Brain-Drain who chortled—most of them cackled.) "I expected you would be coming."

"Your vile plan will never work," responded AI. "I'm here to see that Superopolis will once again experience the amazing benefits of McCavity's Ultra-Paste."

"On the contrary," Professor Brain-Drain corrected. "Without access to McCavity's, the people of Superopolis will soon see their teeth rotting and falling out of their mouths. With no teeth, they won't be able to eat. In their starved, weakened states, it will be easy for me to drain the intelligence from every citizen of Superopolis, absorbing it all into my own brain. I'll become a supergenius!"

How incredibly evil! I was so horrified by Brain-Drain's nasty plot that I ignored how little sense it

NAME: Professor Brain-Drain. **POWER:** The ability to enhance his own intelligence by draining the intelligence of others. **LIMITATIONS:** Has a tendency to overthink things. **CAREER:** Superopolis's most successful criminal mastermind for over fifty years. The Professor has been in semiretirement for over a decade. **CLASSIFICATION:** A major power and a twisted brain make for a lethal combination. His recent inactivity is greatly appreciated.

made. Thank goodness AI was there!

"You obviously didn't count on me," the Amazing Indestructo proclaimed as he bared his brilliant (and indestructible) white teeth.

"Of course I did," replied the Professor matter-of-factly as he pulled a metal box from his lab coat and punched a button on it. "And now I'd like to introduce you to my latest invention. I call them my Robotic Rabbits, and I suggest you be particularly wary of their atomic incisors."

Dozens of metallic bunny rabbits suddenly appeared from all directions. These weren't your ordinary metallic bunnies, either. These bunnies were almost six feet tall! And as if that wasn't bad enough, their front teeth were enormous! In fact, they looked like they could cut through a steel beam. The Amazing Indestructo remained as cool as an indestructible cucumber.

"Is that the best you can do?" he taunted the Professor.

Before the nemesis of niceness could even respond, the Amazing Indestructo picked up the closest Robotic Rabbit by the feet and began swinging it around in a circle. As the others rushed to attack they found themselves being smashed and pulverized. By the time AI stopped his spinning, the rabbit he was holding had been reduced to a blunt hunk of metal. A lot of the attackers had been reduced to pieces as well. But others were still unharmed and not only that, more were joining them every second. In fact, they seemed to be multiplying like . . . well, rabbits!

They swarmed toward AI, and the ones that made it to him began to gnaw at him with their atomic teeth.

"This has no effect on me." AI laughed at Professor Brain-Drain. "Have you forgotten I'm indestructible?"

"Curses! You're right!" the Professor responded.

I find it a bit hard to believe that a genius like Professor Brain-Drain could actually forget something that obvious, but, then again, I guess there wouldn't be a show if he didn't forget it every week.

One by one, the Robotic Rabbits attempted to sink their teeth into the Amazing Indestructo, and one by one, each of their heads exploded. Before long, Professor Brain-Drain's lair was littered with metallic bits of bunnies. The Amazing Indestructo calmly waded through the debris, grabbed the Professor by the collar, and hoisted him into the air.

Just then, who should arrive but the League of Ultimate Goodness. The Crimson Creampuff, huffing and puffing, led the group into the warehouse.

"Here"—*huff puff*—"we"—*huff puff*—"are," he wheezed. "Is there anything"—*huff puff*—"we can do to"—*huff puff*—"help?"

Without waiting for instruction, Spaghetti Man lashed out at one of the headless Robotic Rabbits, spinning strands of spaghetti around its immobile body. The lifeless robot tipped over, and the strands of pasta broke easily, so it came crashing to the ground.

"Where's everybody else?" asked the Amazing Indestructo.

"Well now, pardner," replied Whistlin' Dixie, "Moleman is diggin' his way here. I reckon he'll be poppin' up in pret' near three hours. And Major Bummer is still in the heliocopter, tryin' to get his seat belt undone. If yer int'rested in ma 'pinion, I 'spect the best thing we all could do is get this here McCavity's Ultra-Paste back out to the desperate folk o' Superopolis."

"Good idea, Dixie," AI concurred.

Whistlin' Dixie started whistling the McCavity's Ultra-Paste jingle (in perfect tune, as always) while she and the rest of the leaguers hauled out cases of the toothpaste.

"Meanwhile, I'll deliver this vile villain to prison where he belongs," said AI. "I suspect this is one evil genius who's learned the consequences of not brushing your teeth."

"Or flossing," piped up Professor Brain-Drain just as the final credits began to run across the screen.

Another great episode, I thought to myself. Just then I heard my mom calling me for breakfast. As I got up to turn off the TV, a commercial for McCavity's came on. I never used to like their toothpaste because it sticks to your teeth and sort of tastes like mushrooms, but if AI recommended it, I would have to give it another try.

My ultimate goal is to be just like the Amazing Indestructo—minus the superpower, of course— because, after all, he *is* the greatest hero ever!

CHAPTER TWO

Breakfast of Champions

"OB, it's time to eat," my mom called again just as I came running down the stairs. Mom and Dad both call me OB. I sort of like it, except when my friends are around. All the kids call me "O Boy."

When I came into the kitchen, my mom was holding a pitcher of juice. The icicles that hang in strips from the arms of her powder-blue costume were all jingling against each other.

"Here, honey. Have a glass of orange juice while your father finishes scrambling the eggs."

"It's kind of warm, Mom," I said as she handed me the glass. This is a routine that Mom and I do every morning. She gave a quick wink, and then her eyes focused on the glass. In about two seconds, I felt

NAME: Snowflake. **POWER:** Able to freeze anything just by focusing her gaze on it. **LIMITATIONS:** Objects must be within a radius of a hundred feet. **CAREER:** After a stint with the New Crusaders, Snowflake took a high-level position with the Corpsicle Coolant Corporation. **CLASSIFICATION:** A coolheaded, class act.

NAME: Thermo. **POWER:** The ability to generate intense levels of heat in his hands. **LIMITATIONS:** His power is not always under control. Be careful when shaking hands with Thermo. **CAREER:** A member of the New Crusaders throughout his twenties, Thermo has spent most of the last decade heating the fryers at Dr. Telomere's Potato Chip Factory. **CLASSIFICATION:** An impressive power as long as he doesn't get too hotheaded.

it chill to exactly the right temperature.

"So what was the Amazing Indestructo up to this morning?" my dad asked casually as he balanced the frying pan on the palm of his left hand. "Saving Superopolis again with that group of no-talents?"

Dad doesn't mean to sound bitter, but sometimes he can't help it. The League of Ultimate Goodness has rejected him every time he's attempted to join. He's determined to return to crime fighting, though. Thanks to all the money Mom makes from her job at the coolant laboratory, he was able to quit his job heating the fryers at Dr. Telomere's Potato Chip Factory. Since then, he's devoted all his time to joining a crime-fighting team.

He even bought a new costume! It has a bright-yellow circle in the middle of his chest that gradually turns to orange and then red, making it look like a three-dimensional fireball. The rest of the costume is a brilliant scarlet. He hadn't put on his yellow cape and boots yet this morning, but they make him look even snazzier. As a final touch, Dad also dabs a little gel in his thick red hair and styles it to look like flames. His hands, of course, are always kept bare so he can use his power.

"Don't let it upset you, dear," Mom said calmly as he scooped the scrambled eggs onto our plates. "Could you heat up some water for my tea before you sit down?"

I felt bad for Dad as I watched him fill up the teakettle and then set it on the palm of his hand. He had been pretty hot stuff (no pun intended) when he was younger and part of a popular group of heroes called the New Crusaders.

I found Dad's collection of newspaper clippings once. There were plenty of stories in the gossip columns because of all the super heroines he dated. The papers gave him nicknames like Hot Hands and Hot-to-Trot and things like that. (He doesn't know that I know this stuff!) But he met my mom when she joined the New Crusaders, and that part of his life changed forever. They fell in love and both retired from crime fighting.

I know he misses it, though, and I really hope he gets into the League one of these days. Then I might get to meet AI!

"I know you want to join," my mother consoled him, "but maybe the Amazing Indestructo just doesn't remember what a successful hero you used to be."

"How could anyone have forgotten"—and here Dad switched to his best booming superhero voice— "the awesome power of Thermo!" Unfortunately, the teakettle resting on his hand began to whistle at exactly the same moment.

"You'll have your chance again, dear," Mom said

as he poured the boiling water into her teacup. "Opportunity comes when you least expect it."

"I sure hope so," he said dejectedly. He ripped open a bag of Dr. Telomere's X-tra Crispy Potato Chips and filled the potato chip bowl that always sat in the center of our table. "Uh-oh, this is our last bag. I'll have to go to the grocery store today."

As he sat down, my mother and I both took a handful of chips and crushed them, sprinkling the crumbs on top of our scrambled eggs. There's no meal that you can't improve with potato chips!

Later that afternoon, while I was playing with my Amazing Indestructo action figure and his Fortress of Rectitude play set, Dad called up to see if I wanted to go to the store with him.

"Absolutely," I shouted back.

I *love* going to the grocery store! Especially with Dad, who never argues about anything I want to buy. Dad was at the front door, ready to go, but as I reached the bottom of the stairs, Mom appeared with a list.

"This is everything we need," she said. "I know you two go overboard every time I send you to the store together, so I'm making a new rule. Besides the items on this list, you're only allowed to purchase two things of your own choosing. Got that? Two! Now have a good time, boys."

It was a typical busy Saturday afternoon at the Mighty Mart. ("It's mighty smart, shopping at the Mighty Mart," says their jingle.) Dad and I started off in the produce section. I had to handle all the fruits and vegetables. If Dad did that, he might accidentally cook them on the spot. Dad never meant to turn fresh tomatoes into sun-dried tomatoes, but it had happened before. We were being watched carefully by the store manager, Mr. Mister. His mouth was open wide as he breathed a fine watery mist onto a section of lettuces, but his eyes were fixed on Dad.

The next aisle was baked goods, and both our eyes lit up. Dad is a huge fan of Maximizer Power Cakes. He believes their creamy center fillings enhance his powers, or "maximize" them, as their ads claim. In reality, I think they only maximize Dad's waistline. A few feet away I spotted the entire line of Amazing Indestructo Doughnut Hole Heroes. They came in a dozen different varieties!

I had no idea which to choose. My favorite was Cinnamon Cyclone. But I also loved Blueberry Bonanza. What to do? Then I spotted the Doughnut Hole Heroes Hodgepodge Assortment: All Twelve Varieties in One Box! Grabbing it from the shelf, I returned to the cart just as Dad was about to set a box of cherry-flavored Maximizer Power Cakes in it.

"This will use up both our choices," he said.

"We should put one of them back," I suggested.

"You can have some of my Power Cakes," he offered.

"I don't like cherry," I replied, holding my ground. "But mine is a variety pack. There's something for everyone in here."

Dad had no good response to my superior logic. I could tell he was flustered because his fingers were starting to leave singe marks on the box of Power Cakes. I also saw Mr. Mister following us with narrowed eyes.

"Okay," Dad finally said, glancing over at the nosy store manager. "We'll take them both for now and figure it out later."

In the next aisle we ran into one of Dad's old friends.

"BB! How's it going?" Dad said. "I haven't seen you in ages."

Dad and the Big Bouncer went way back to when they were both part of the New Crusaders. The Big Bouncer is about as round as he is tall, but that's perfect for his power. Anyone who comes after him just bounces right off. Even better, with something to push off against, he can go bouncing in any direction. He has a kid in my grade named Cannonball, who, unlike his dad, plows through things instead of bouncing off them. He's also unlike his father in that he's kind of a creep.

"Hi, Thermo. Hi, Ordinary Boy. It's good to see you," he said, trying to sound cheerful, even though he looked miserable. "I'm working here now. I was turned down again by the League of Ultimate Goodness. And, of course, none of the younger teams has any interest in an older guy like me."

"Don't I know it," my father agreed. "They gave me the brush-off, too, just a few weeks ago."

The Big Bouncer picked up a case of canned carrots and plopped down on his butt. He immediately bounced up about ten feet and set the case on the top shelf. He landed back on his feet without missing a beat.

"I just don't get it. We used to be the best. Now here I am stocking the shelves at the Mighty Mart."

NAME: Big Bouncer, The. **POWER:** Rubbery and round, the Big Bouncer has skills remarkably similar to those of an elastic ball. **LIMITATIONS:** Often a victim of the three laws of motion. **CAREER:** A founding member of the New Crusaders, his crime-fighting career never rebounded after the team's retirement. **CLASSIFICATION:** There's always a chance of this hero bouncing back.

"Don't worry, BB," my dad said as we continued with our shopping. "Things will work out . . . somehow."

The next aisle had candy on one side and things like nuts and popcorn on the other. I grabbed a large bag of SugarJolt Chocolate Energy Pills and Dad picked up a multipack of Turkey Jerky Rinds. We both knew there was no hope of compromise here.

"Let's just put them in the cart for now," Dad said.

The next section was the first of the two potato chip aisles. This one contained nothing but one-pound bags of original flavor Dr. Telomere's X-tra Crispy Potato Chips. When Dad worked at the factory we got all our potato chips for free. Now we have to buy them like everybody else. Mom's list said to get thirteen bags. We filled up the cart with ten regular bags and then tried to decide which special varieties to choose this week.

My current favorite is the popcorn-flavored chips, while Mom likes the barbecue-flavored variety of Telomere's crinkle-cut style. Dad, as usual, could not make up his mind. I knew that it would be a good fifteen minutes before he decided, so I headed over to the comic book rack.

I was just getting to the good part in the newest issue of *The Amazing Indestructo* (and the League of Ultimate Goodness) when all of a sudden the Mighty Mart was rocked by an enormous muffled explosion.

DR. TELOMERE'S POTATO CHIP FACTORY:

Superopolis's most successful business by far, the Dr. Telomere's brand of potato chips has become a staple in every home thanks to their perpetual crunch and their all-around salty, fried goodness. The Dr. Telomere's factory is located at the base of the Carbunkle Mountains within the confines of sprawling Telomere Park. Most people assume that Dr. Telomere is a fictional character created as a marketing device to sell potato chips, although rumors of a genuine Dr. Telomere still persist.

CHAPTER THREE

Mayhem at the Mighty Mart

As I ran toward the explosion (after all, that's what superheroes do) I noticed other heroes from all over the store converging on the paper products aisle. I couldn't believe what I saw when I got there. A villain was on a rampage!

"No one will ridicule the Multiplier ever again," the criminal screeched, pitching rolls of toilet paper at everyone.

I immediately pulled out my *Li'l Hero's Handbook* and looked him up. Sure enough, there was an entry on a villain called the Multiplier.

According to the book, the problem for the Multiplier was that he just couldn't make duplicates fast enough to cause any real harm. And he could only

NAME: Multiplier, The. **POWER:** Has the ability to make an exact duplicate of anything he touches. **LIMITATIONS:** Power works slowly and only on small items. **CAREER:** Turned briefly and ineffectively to crime in his late teens; inactive ever since. **CLASSIFICATION:** Minuscule threat.

duplicate small things. If he tried duplicating a car, for instance, he might end up with a fender or a steering wheel or maybe just a dipstick. As a result, his crimes had all been fairly small (duplicating stamps, making copies of winning lottery tickets—that sort of thing), and the *Li'l Hero's Handbook* classified him as a minuscule threat—possibly the most embarrassing thing that could be said about a supervillain.

Somehow that had all changed. As I watched him multiplying rolls of toilet paper out of control, I knew he must have figured out a way to speed up his power.

Behind the Multiplier, the paper products aisle was now hopelessly clogged. It didn't look like the Multiplier even needed to touch the rolls to create duplicates. Then, over the sounds of the commotion, I heard metal groaning. It took me a moment to realize that it was caused by the pressure of all those rolls of toilet paper building up in the aisle with no place to go.

"Tremble before the awesome power of the Multiplier," the villain shrieked in that way that only a previously powerless person can.

There was a moment of almost complete silence as both the villain and the heroes surrounding him paused and looked back at the mountain of toilet paper. Suddenly, the long shelves on either side of the

aisle gave way. The metallic groan grew louder and louder, and then all at once the shelves creaked and buckled and finally toppled over. Heroes, in a very unheroic way, began screaming and running as the shelves on both sides of the paper products aisle flopped over in both directions. This started a chain reaction as those shelves crashed against other shelves like falling dominos.

"Hey, you guys," I shouted to the throngs of fleeing heroes. "Shouldn't you be rushing to the rescue rather than running away like cowards?"

That was all the guilt it took. Heroes paused for just a moment before turning to face the threat. Some went to the aid of trapped shoppers while others did what they could to stop the tumbling shelves. But it wasn't easy. The release of all that built-up pressure had caused the toilet paper rolls to explode into the air, and they were now raining down on everyone.

The heroes not focused on the cascading shelves were having even less luck dealing with either the toilet paper, which now seemed to be everywhere, or the Multiplier, who continued creating more rolls which he launched with pinpoint accuracy at the helpless superheroes. I felt completely powerless, which wasn't unusual for me, but then I was distracted by a familiar voice behind me.

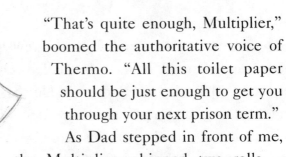

"That's quite enough, Multiplier," boomed the authoritative voice of Thermo. "All this toilet paper should be just enough to get you through your next prison term."

As Dad stepped in front of me, the Multiplier whipped two rolls directly at him. Thermo never blinked. Instead he caught both of them, one in each hand. His hands began to glow red, and both rolls of toilet paper burst into flames.

Before the Multiplier knew what was happening, the two flaming rolls were hurtling back in his direction. As the Multiplier ducked to get out of their way, he tripped and stumbled into a pile of toilet paper. He struggled to his feet with his cape now in flames. Then, before he could launch another attack, a large rolling object came rumbling up behind him at full speed.

"The Big Bouncer!" my dad said with an enormous grin.

The Multiplier had only half a second to turn and

look before the shelf-stocking superhero smashed into him. The Big Bouncer came to a stop, and everyone in the store watched in amazement as the villain went sailing across the front checkout area like a flaming comet. At the top of his arc, I saw something small drop from his hands and fall to the floor. But the Multiplier continued on, finally crashing smack into a huge pyramid of onions all the way over in Produce and knocking himself unconscious. Mr. Mister stepped up to him and blew a fine mist over the flaming villain until the fire was out. He gave my dad an irritated look.

Meanwhile, I ran toward the object that the Multiplier had dropped. But before I could get to it, I heard a rumble coming from the ceiling above me. Everybody rushed to get out of the way as something crashed through the roof. In the cloud of debris, all I could see was a foot landing right on the object that the Multiplier had dropped, smashing it to bits.

Then, as the smoke and dust cleared, all my curiosity about the object vanished in an instant.

Because standing there, right before my very eyes, was the Amazing Indestructo himself! Live and in person! The smoke was coming from his rocket pack. I was frozen with awe. He shut off his rocket blasters and turned toward the unconscious Multiplier.

"No one panic," he said in that powerful voice I'd know anywhere. "I can handle this dastardly deed doer."

Before my dad or the Big Bouncer could say anything, the Amazing Indestructo pulled the crumpled villain from the pile of onions and hauled him back to the spot beneath the hole in the roof.

"And while you're shopping, folks, remember that the Amazing Indestructo brand of dishwashing detergent is *invulnerable* to grease!" With that he started up his rocket pack and blasted back through the roof, taking the still-unconscious Multiplier with him. The customers in the store erupted in applause and then stampeded their way to the cleaning products aisle.

"But we had already taken care of him," Dad said. The Big Bouncer just gave a resigned shrug. I didn't pay much attention, though. I was too amazed at actually seeing AI in person! Then something else caught my attention. Near the checkout lane at register eleven: The Amazing Indestructo Collector Card Series Number One. "Collect all sixty-four!" a burst proclaimed on the box. My hands shook as I lifted one of the packs. Each pack cost a dollar, so I could buy five, which I quickly did.

Putting the packs in one of my pockets, I went back to Dad, who was glumly checking through the items in our cart, just to make sure we hadn't forgotten something in the confusion.

"We still have a problem," he said. "We've picked out four items for ourselves, but your mother will only allow two."

It was then, as the store cleanup crew arrived to start picking up onions, patching the hole in the ceiling, and fixing the disaster in the paper products aisle, that I had a brilliant idea.

"She said we were only allowed to pick out two items, right?" I asked.

"That's right," my dad said warily.

"Well, so the Doughnut Hole Heroes and the SugarJolt Chocolate Energy Pills are my two, and the Maximizer Power Cakes and Turkey Jerky Rinds are your two. If she had meant two items total, she should have said we were allowed one item each. I would think that when she said two items, she meant that we *each* were allowed two items."

"OB, you're a genius." My dad's mood lifted slightly as he mussed up my hair. It was nice, but I had to push his hand away before he accidentally set my hair on fire like that time when I was six.

As we were having everything rung up, the other members of the League of Ultimate Goodness finally arrived. I spotted Major Bummer, Whistlin' Dixie, and the Crimson Creampuff immediately. Most of them were out of breath, and they all looked a little confused.

"Don't bother, guys," Mr. Mister informed them. "AI handled everything."

That comment was enough to send my dad back into a funk. But I was focused on my new cards. I didn't even realize until later that Mr. Mister's cleanup crew had swept up the fragments of whatever the Multiplier had dropped.

As we headed out of the store, I heard a thump coming from the pavement. *Thump, thump.* And then, farther away: *thump, thump.* After about the tenth thump, I saw the Moleman's head burst through a small grassy island in the parking lot.

"You're too late," my father said in disgust, not even glancing down at the muddled-looking member of the League of Ultimate Goodness. "The Amazing Indestructo has already saved the day."

I should have been more supportive of my dad in his gloomy mood. After all, I knew he and the Big

Bouncer had taken down the Multiplier and gotten none of the credit. But I was distracted. I had five packets of cards in my back pocket, and I couldn't wait to get home and open them.

CHAPTER FOUR

Counting Cards

Mom was incredibly irritated about the two additional items that somehow ended up as four. So I left the house immediately after breakfast on Sunday and headed straight for the headquarters of my team, the Junior Leaguers, for our regularly scheduled weekly emergency meeting.

Okay, "headquarters" might be a bit of an exaggeration. Our regular meeting place is a tree house in Stench's backyard. But it's a really *cool* tree house. Stench's dad, Windbag, owns a junkyard. In fact, Stench's entire yard is really just one enormous pile of junk. As a result, his dad was able to put together all sorts of weird things to make a tree house with practically everything a kid could want. It has electricity, heating and air-conditioning, a game room, a pantry that's always stocked with potato chips, and a refrigerator full of things to drink.

Stench says his dad built the place for him because of what a good kid he is. I think the real reason was to keep him outside instead of stinking up the house. Don't get me wrong. Stench is a great guy and one of the strongest heroes I know, even though he's still just a kid. But, man, can he clear a room.

I would never hold it against him, though. Not after the amazing friend he's been to me. We met in kindergarten. On the very first day, I was getting picked on because of my lack of a superpower by Cannonball. Like I mentioned earlier, Cannonball is the son of the Big Bouncer and he's a real jerk.

On day one, Cannonball was threatening to roll right over me, when up steps this kid who was big enough to be a third grader. He was wearing an open orange vest with lots of pockets and matching orange pants. The pants had rows of canisters attached up and down the sides by small straps.

"It's not nice to pick on others," he said, stepping right up to Cannonball.

"Why don't you go play with the rest of the ten-year-olds?" Cannonball mocked him, not letting go of me.

"I'm in kindergarten just like you," the new kid said as he reached for Cannonball's arm—the one holding me by the collar. "Now why don't you let go of my friend here."

I had never seen him before, but at that moment I was more than happy to have him as a friend. He barely squeezed Cannonball's wrist and the round little creep started hollering. He backed off for a moment, and then his face turned red as he got really angry.

"Okay, so you've been held back a few years," snorted Cannonball, "but that doesn't mean I can't still flatten you."

"Just because I'm big doesn't mean I was held back," my new friend informed Cannonball, even as the bully came barreling toward him. "But it does mean I can pound the potato chips out of you if I have to."

And, sure enough, he grabbed Cannonball and hoisted him straight into the air. No one was more surprised than Cannonball himself, who immediately began to yell in panic.

"So what do you think we should do with him?" The stranger turned to me, a mischievous grin on his face.

I looked around the playground and saw something that gave me a great idea.

"I think he might enjoy the seesaw," I said, returning his grin.

NAME: Stench. **POWER:** Incredible superstrength.
LIMITATIONS: Sadly, a regrettable side effect of this power has led to this young hero's unfortunate name. **CAREER:** The strongest kid by far at Watson Elementary and a member of the Junior Leaguers.
CLASSIFICATION: A remarkable power as long as you're standing upwind.

"Great idea." He laughed. "Let's give him a ride."

I followed him as he carried the screaming Cannonball over to the seesaw. With no effort at all, he tossed Cannonball onto the far side and then jumped onto the nearer side. We both watched with satisfaction as Cannonball went flying off across the playground, his wail fading along with him.

"Kids always make fun of me because of my size," he said as he stuck out his hand to me, "but usually only once. My name is Stench, by the way."

The second he said it I found out how he got his name. I shook his hand anyway.

"My name is Ordinary Boy," I replied, my eyes watering from the smell. "That's because I don't have any kind of power."

"My power is my strength," Stench said. He pulled one of the canisters from a loop on his pants leg and began spraying it to neutralize the odor. "The problem is that my strength sometimes shows itself in unpleasant ways. I'll make you a deal. I won't make fun of you if you won't make fun of me."

"It's a deal," I replied. And we've been best friends ever since.

Climbing up the ladder, I could tell by the faint but lingering smell that Stench was already there.

As I entered the clubhouse through the hole in the

center of the floor, I didn't see anyone at first. Then I noticed a bushy clump of blond hair poking over the back of the couch. I peeked over and saw Halogen Boy. He was munching from a bowl of potato chips sitting in his lap and appeared hypnotized by what he was watching on the television. I slowly began waving my hand like a pendulum directly in front of his face. His eyes, hidden behind the dark goggles he always wore, finally appeared to focus on my waving hand.

"Hey, O Boy. You're just in time," he said, momentarily glowing as brightly as the TV screen in front of him. "AI is just coming on."

"Excellent," I responded, and I plopped down on the end of the couch right next to our Hall of Trophies. Well, to be honest, it really wasn't a hall. In fact it was just an empty aquarium turned upside down. So far, it contained only a doorknob, a sardine can, and a cocktail umbrella, but we had high hopes for its future.

Just then I heard the refrigerator door close. I glanced over to the kitchen area and saw Stench.

"Hi, O Boy," he said as he handed Halogen Boy a bottle of apple juice. "Can I get you one, too?"

Hal (that's what we all call him) poured the juice from the bottle into the sippy cup that he always carried. It was attached to his belt loop by an elastic strap. We kid him all the time about still having a sippy cup, but it actually makes a lot of sense. His ability to glow gets a lot stronger the more apple juice he drinks. Don't ask me why. Orange juice, lemonade, soda pop—nothing else had any effect, but apple juice could get him glowing like a firefly. The sippy cup was just an easy way to always keep some handy.

"Sure. I'll take one, too," I replied. It took me a moment to realize that Stench was sporting a big bushy mustache the same brownish color as the hair on his head. "Um, and what's with the mustache?"

"Guess who." He snorted with disgust.

Stench's older brother, Fuzz Boy, has the ability to grow hair on anything he touches. When he was a baby his parents thought that he would become a zillionaire by growing hair for bald people. The problem is that the hair only lasts for about six hours. So, stuck with a fairly useless power, he spends most of his time using it to play pranks—mostly on his younger brother.

"He did it this morning before breakfast," Stench grumbled. "So it should be gone in a couple of hours."

"What should be gone?"

The three of us all turned to see Plasma Girl coming up through the floor of the tree house. Well, actually, "oozing up" would be more correct. Plasma Girl can change herself into a gelatin-like glob and this allows her to get into all sorts of places in ways that most people can't. She never climbs up the ladder to the tree house. Instead, she turns into her goopy state and slithers along a ventilation shaft or up the trunk. It only takes her a few seconds to switch back into her normal body. She doesn't have a costume in the conventional sense, since she would lose it every time she used her power, but her skin produces a constantly shifting plasma covering from neck to toes. Its colors tend to be blue, purple, and pink and it's really cool and iridescent.

"We were talking about Stench's mustache," Halogen Boy and I both said helpfully.

"I think it looks good on you, Stench," Plasma Girl said, giving it a playful tug. "You should consider growing it back in about ten years."

"No way," he responded. "Want an apple juice?"

"Thanks," Plasma Girl said. "Where's Tadpole? It's not like him to be the last one here."

Just then, as if on cue, Tadpole poked his head through the opening in the floor.

"Here I am, guys," he said as he climbed up, "and I have a very good reason for being late. I've just spent the morning with the coolest thing ever invented so far in the history of the universe."

"What is it?" we all asked.

"The Amazing Indestructo Collector Cards," he

revealed proudly. He pulled a small stack of cards from a compartment on the olive-green utility belt he wore on top of his camouflage leotards. "They've just been released!"

"I know," I said. "I bought five packs yesterday and I brought them with me."

"Me, too," Stench added. "I have five packs, too."

Tadpole looked disappointed. He likes to think he's the first to find anything out. But then Hal distracted him.

"Those look really neat," Hal said softly. The apple juice he had just drunk produced a bright glow and we all had to close our eyes. "Oops. Sorry about that."

"There's sixty-four of them all together," Tadpole said, like we didn't already know. "I was thinking we should try and complete the set as a team."

"This isn't going to be your new excuse to get out of my afternoon tea party, is it?" asked Plasma Girl suspiciously. "You've wiggled out of it three times now, and this time you promised."

As you can probably tell, Plasma Girl doesn't hang out with us because she's a tomboy or anything. Just the opposite, actually. We all met her for the first time in second grade, and, believe me, nothing impresses a second-grade boy like a girl who can turn herself into a bubbling mass of ectoplasm and slither across a playground. The first time she did it, we practically begged her to join our group. It was only later that we realized she was into the usual lame stuff that most girls like.

I'll admit, we had doubts at first. But then we decided, why not? We're modern, freethinking guys, after all. And, besides, we all realized that even when she wasn't an oozing, bubbling puddle of goop, she was still pretty cool. She'd have to be for us to agree to be guests at her tea parties. And although you'll never hear me admit this in front of the guys, she's kept us from doing a lot of stupid things over the years.

"Tea parties are so lame," Tadpole muttered in his usual undiplomatic way.

"And you're coming to one this afternoon." She glared at Tadpole but spoke to all of us. "Aren't you?"

"We promise," we all said robotically.

We eagerly began spreading out the cards on the table in front of the couch.

"Hey, Tadpole, you want an apple juice?" Stench asked. "Everybody else already has one."

"Thanks, Stench, but I can get it," Tadpole responded. Without even lifting his head from the cards, his tongue whipped from his mouth, snaked into the kitchen, looped itself around the refrigerator door handle, and yanked it open. Tadpole wrapped his tongue around a bottle of apple juice, used it to nudge the door shut, and reeled it all the way back—all without looking. As his tongue released the bottle and it dropped into his hand, the last of the cards were laid out on the table.

"This is incredible," he said excitedly. "Two cards per pack, so we have ten from O Boy, ten from Stench, and sixteen from me."

The first thing we noticed as we oohed and aahed over the cards was how many of them were pictures of the Amazing Indestructo. They weren't all duplicates, either. There were just lots of different images of AI. We counted twenty-two in all. After looking them over carefully, we realized that eight of them were duplicates, leaving us with fourteen unique AI cards. The remaining fourteen cards were split evenly between members of the League of Ultimate Goodness and some of AI's greatest enemies.

We had seven members of LUG: Major Bummer, the Bee Lady, Mannequin, the Human Compass, and Lord Pincushion, plus two more duplicates of Major Bummer. The seven villain cards were those for the Prophetess, Reverso, the Iconoclast, two copies of Cyclotron's card, and two cards for a mysterious villain named the Sneak. We'd heard of him before but had never seen a picture. The card did little to clear

NAME: Plasma Girl. **POWER:** Able to transform herself into a gelatinous goo. **LIMITATIONS:** Gelatinous goo has few practical uses. **CAREER:** First and only female member of the Junior Leaguers. **CLASSIFICATION:** A moderate power put to exceptional use.

up the mystery. All that was visible was a pale outline of a person who had blended in with the pattern of the wall behind him. You could only sort of see his eyes.

What really mattered, though, was that all together we had twenty-four unique cards.

"If there are sixty-four total, that means we still need . . ." Halogen Boy's goggles tipped downward to where his fingers were attempting to count out the answer.

"We still need a whole bunch of cards," Tadpole said with annoyance.

The rest of us were annoyed, too, but not at the thought of finding the remaining cards. We were annoyed because the clubhouse suddenly started to stink.

"Oh my goodness!" Plasma Girl cried, frantically waving both hands in front of her face.

"Can't you do that somewhere else?" Tadpole asked.

"Sorry." Stench blushed. "It comes on pretty suddenly."

"Let's get out of here, anyway," I suggested. "I think it's time to head over to the Mighty Mart. After all, we have a collection to complete!"

CHAPTER FIVE

A Bright Idea

When we got to the store, the first things I noticed were the displays of toilet paper that were everywhere. They all had signs offering huge discounts. Buy one, get five free—that sort of thing. The ceiling that AI had crashed through had already been completely repaired and the shelves had been raised back up.

We went straight to the checkout lanes with the card packs. In lane one there was a box that still had about a dozen packs in it.

"How many of these can we afford to buy?" asked Tadpole. "I only have three dollars left after what I bought earlier today."

I did a little calculating in my head.

"Well, we need forty more cards," I said for starters.

"So far, of the first thirty-six cards we bought, twelve of them, or one third, were duplicates, and twenty-four, or two-thirds, were unique. If that ratio stays the same, we'd have to buy . . . hmm, let me think."

Actually, I knew the answer right away, but I didn't want the group to think I was a math geek or something, so I pretended like it took me a while to get the answer.

"We'd have to buy at least sixty cards in order to have even a small chance of getting the forty individual cards that we need," I finally announced. "In reality, as we get closer to completing the set, our rate of success will drop even further and it will take even more to find the last few we need. Sixty should be our target for now, though."

"I'd love to know how you do that," Stench said as he shook his head. Plasma Girl just gave me a wink and a smile. I hoped none of the guys saw it.

"At two per pack, that's thirty packs we'd need to buy," Tadpole said with a sigh. "Like I said, I only have three dollars."

"I think I have five," Stench said.

"Me, too," agreed Plasma Girl. "But I need it to buy scones for the tea party."

"I only have two," Halogen Boy said sadly as he stuck a finger in his pocket to illuminate its interior.

"And I have five," I added. "That gives us a total of twenty dollars."

"What about my scones?" asked an irritated Plasma Girl.

"Can we just have potato chips with the tea?" I asked plaintively.

"Oh, fine," she relented. "So we have enough for forty cards. And we need exactly forty cards. . . ."

"But how can we find the packs that have just the cards we need?" Halogen Boy asked. Instinctively, his hand reached for his sippy cup and he took a drink, glowing brighter with frustration.

"I think I have an idea," I announced. I picked up one of the card packs. "Hal, stick out your hand."

I placed the pack flat on the palm of his hand and said, "Now make yourself as bright as you can."

He took another drink from his sippy cup and began to glow. His white costume looks

solid, but in reality it's made out of a tight mesh material that allows his light to pass through unobstructed. The same wasn't true for his green briefs, boots and cape, but that hardly seemed to matter. The light he was generating continued to get brighter until the others had to turn away. I cupped my hands over my eyes and focused on the pack of cards. Sure enough, as he reached a strong enough wattage, I clearly caught a glimpse of a card featuring AI that I hadn't seen before, and a card with another member of LUG—Spaghetti Man. Then, Hal's hand got even brighter and I lost the image. In fact, I was now seeing the bones in his hand as clearly as an X-ray.

"Too much," I said squinting my eyes shut. Halogen Boy dialed it back to the point where I could see the cards inside the pack. I told everyone what they were and we set it aside to buy.

"You're a genius," Plasma Girl said with admiration. I couldn't help it—I blushed almost as brightly as Halogen Boy.

With Hal and a full sippy cup, we went from pack to pack and aisle to aisle, avoiding lots of packs that were filled with duplicates. We found some packs that had a card we needed, but if the other card was one we already owned, we'd skip it and move on. By the time we got to checkout lane nine, we had nineteen packs with thirty-eight of the forty cards we still needed. By this time, though, we had attracted some unwanted attention.

Mr. Mister was waiting in lane ten. He watched us suspiciously as I picked up the first pack and set it in Hal's hand. It wasn't like we were doing anything illegal, so I tried to ignore him and told Hal to light up. Like most of the packs we were finding now, it had two duplicates. I could feel a fine mist settling down on my shoulders as I handed Hal the next pack. Mr. Mister was clearly annoyed, mostly because he couldn't think of any technical reason to throw us out of the store. I just turned to him and shrugged. He always seems annoyed about something. Maybe it's because he has a crappy power. But, come on,

give me a break. I don't have *any* power, but I still try to be a nice person.

As Hal's hand lit up I saw a card with a character named Meteor Boy on it.

"Who is Meteor Boy?" I said aloud. The rest of the team just shook their heads, confused. This was very strange, but there was no time to discuss it. The mist gathering around the store manager's head made him look all steamed up—which, of course, he was. The card sharing the pack was an AI image that none of us could remember seeing before.

"Okay, guys, I think we have 'em all!" I said quickly.

"Well, then," Mr. Mister said, with a look on his face that reminded me of the short-lived disastrous pickle-flavored potato chips that Dr. Telomere's had released last year, "if you're going to buy those, I suggest you do so and stop clogging my checkout lanes."

We did exactly that, and were soon back at our headquarters. As Plasma Girl got her tea party ready, we unwrapped the twenty packs and spread them out on the table. Of course we didn't expect any surprises, but we got one anyway. The AI card in the final pack we had bought was identical to one of the ones we had found earlier that morning. With Mr. Mister hovering over us we had rushed into making a mistake. We only had sixty-three cards. One was still missing.

CHAPTER SIX

The Mystery of Meteor Boy

That night at home, all I could think about was the one card we were missing. The most frustrating part was that I didn't even know who was pictured on it. Normally, I would have guessed it was another Amazing Indestructo. But so far the deck had had thirty-two of them—exactly half the total. It only seemed logical for that to be all of them. That meant that the missing card was either a member of the League of Ultimate Goodness or one of AI's villains.

Now it would also seem logical for the remaining thirty-two cards to be divided into sixteen heroes and sixteen villains. I knew fifteen we had were members of LUG, and another fifteen were villains. And then there was Meteor Boy. Was he a hero or a villain? Young villains were unusual but not unheard-of. In fact, there were some creeps in my class who I'd bet were well on their way to becoming villains.

I pulled out my copy of the *Li'l Hero's Handbook* and looked up Meteor Boy. Sure enough, there was a listing with the same picture as the card.

One mission? Missing in action? So why would this kid have gotten his own trading card? When Dad came up to tuck me in, I decided to pick his brain.

"Time for bed, OB," he said.

"Okay, Dad." The night air had cooled my room quite a bit. With a shiver, I got my AI pajamas from my dresser drawer.

Dad pulled back the covers on my bed and ran his hands back and forth across the sheet. "Okay, hero, it's all set."

"Dad?" I asked as I crawled under the sheets, where it was now warm and toasty.

"What is it, OB?"

"Have you ever heard of Meteor Boy?"

Dad paused a moment, and I could instantly tell by the look on his face that he had.

"Yes," he said finally. "I haven't heard that name in quite a while—almost twenty-five years, in fact."

"Who is he?"

"Well, he first came on the scene when I was a

LI'L HERO'S HANDBOOK
★ PEOPLE ★

NAME: Meteor Boy. **POWER:** The ability to fly really, really fast. **LIMITATIONS:** But not fast enough. **CAREER:** Meteor Boy performed only one known mission. **CLASSIFICATION:** Missing in action.

teenager. He was younger than I was, though, as you'd guess by the name Meteor Boy. At the time, all the major superheroes were going through a phase where it was trendy to take on young kids as sidekicks. A hero would look for a kid about your age who had a power that was similar to, or complemented, his own power."

"What do you mean, Dad?" I asked.

"For instance, there was a hero, who is gone now, called the Zephyr."

"I know about him!" I responded, remembering the card for him that we had found as part of our morning haul. "He's one of the original members of the League of Ultimate Goodness."

"Exactly," my father continued. "He was able to control the winds and manipulate them to do whatever he liked. He had a sidekick named Funnel Boy, who could spin himself into a funnel cloud. The two made a pretty good team."

"I get it," I said. The idea sounded pretty cool to me.

"Of course, this was about when the Amazing Indestructo became such a star," my father added.

"Wow! Tell me about that!" Of course I knew everything about AI, but I was always eager to hear it again.

"Well, AI was just starting to

make a name for himself, but he already considered himself the city's most powerful hero. Naturally, he thought he should also have a sidekick."

"Naturally," I agreed, instantly thinking how awesome it would be to have that role. I also wondered why I had never heard about this.

"And, of course," my father continued, "he thought his sidekick should be the most powerful of all sidekicks.

That's when he discovered Meteor Boy."

"Tell me about him," I asked.

"When he met AI, he wasn't much older than you are now. But he already had an incredible power. He could streak through the skies with the speed of a meteor. As you know, there aren't a lot of heroes who can travel through the air, and those who do have a tremendous advantage."

"That's why AI uses a jet pack," I volunteered.

"That's right," my dad agreed. "So he knew an impressive ability when he saw it. Meteor Boy was still young, though, and he hadn't really mastered his power yet."

"What a great power to have," I said, wide-eyed. Personally, I'd be thrilled to have any power at all. Dad caught my change of mood right away.

"Be careful what you wish for," he said. "Things didn't turn out well for Meteor Boy."

"What happened?" I asked, even though I wasn't sure I wanted to hear the answer.

"He just wasn't ready. The Amazing Indestructo was a rookie, too. He took Meteor Boy into a situation that was too big for both of them. Back then, Professor Brain-Drain was fully active and by far the worst of the supervillains, and AI wanted to start right at the top. Of course, AI was indestructible.

The problem was that Meteor Boy wasn't."

"So . . . ?" I couldn't finish the sentence.

"Let's just say no one knows exactly what happened to him," my father concluded.

"That's what it says in my handbook, too," I confirmed. "But he was a hero, right?"

"Oh, yes, but in a way that no one had counted on. It was his example that made everyone recognize the incredible danger they were putting these young kids into. Shortly after the incident with Meteor Boy, kids went back to being kids, and adult superheroes went back to fighting crime on their own."

Dad leaned over to kiss my forehead and then stood up.

"I know it's tempting to get out there and start doing everything you can as soon as you can," he said as he clicked off the light, "but don't pass up the opportunity to enjoy being a kid, too."

As the door closed, I stared silently into the darkness of my room. I heard what my father had said, but to be perfectly honest all I could think about was what it would be like to be the Amazing Indestructo's sidekick. I couldn't imagine anything cooler! But who was I kidding? AI would never pick a sidekick with no power whatsoever. And if a kid with such an incredible power couldn't handle teaming with AI, then what chance would I have? I know Dad didn't mean it that way, but it sure managed to depress me.

The only good news was that in the information about Meteor Boy, I had also found the answer to my main question. I knew who was on the missing card.

CHAPTER SEVEN

Less Is More

The next day, I walked into class before the bell rang and ducked when I saw Cannonball and Lobster Boy with erasers in their hands (or claws, in the case of Lobster Boy). They were waiting to throw them at whoever came through the door, but when they saw it was me, they stopped themselves at the last second. Cannonball has never gotten any nicer to me over the last five years, but he knows better than to pick on me.

The kid who came in after me wasn't so lucky. It was the Spore, and as he stepped into the room, two erasers smacked him right in the face, raising a cloud of mold spores and chalk dust. Well, it could have been worse. He had only been hit by the two erasers Cannonball had thrown. In his excitement, Lobster Boy ended up snapping his erasers in half with his claws, producing a second cloud of chalk dust around his own head. Then, before any of the dust could settle to the ground, in walked the Human Sponge. The cloud of mold and chalk wafting around the Spore was absorbed into her before she even knew what was happening.

"Ewww, that is so disgusting," she complained. "Somebody wring my head."

"Gladly!" I heard Cannonball say gleefully as I made my way to my desk.

The rest of my teammates were already at their desks. They were still racking their brains trying to figure out the person on the missing card.

"I say that it's the Mimic, who got kicked out of the League of Ultimate Goodness ten years ago for doing AI impersonations behind his back," insisted Tadpole.

"No, he's too obscure," Plasma Girl disagreed, only half paying attention as she painted her nails with a glittery silver polish that matched her costume. "It's probably just another pose of AI."

"What about the Weatherman?" Stench suggested. "He was a LUG for a little while. I never could figure out why they didn't keep him. I mean, the guy can manipulate the weather! What more could they want?!"

"We could ask Puddle Boy," Hal suggested.

Stench turned toward Puddle Boy, who sat two rows over, near the wall.

"Hey, Puddle Boy," hollered Stench, "did they put your dad's picture in the new set of AI Collector Cards?"

Much to the Weatherman's constant embarrassment, his son's only power was the ability to create puddles beneath his feet. Even now, the pressure of having to answer a question was causing one to form. The Human Sponge, who was on her way to her desk after having her head wrung out by Cannonball, warily avoided it, while the Banshee, who sat behind Puddle Boy, let out a piercing scream as she scooted her desk away.

"No," he answered self-consciously as the wail subsided. "They called and asked him if they could, but he threatened to sue them if they did. Then he said a whole bunch of words that I don't think I should repeat. I don't think my dad likes AI very much."

"Well, that'th out," said Tadpole. His tongue was wrapped around a pencil he was sharpening halfway across the room. "We might ath well jutht keep looking."

"You sound just like Melonhead." Plasma Girl giggled.

"Who thoundth like me?"

We all turned to see Melonhead come into the

room. This kid had a head that literally looked like a melon. I don't mean it was green or anything, but it was bald, shaped like a melon, and had wavy lines running down the sides of his face like the markings on a watermelon. And every time he spoke he spit seeds all over the place. Despite having a power that's almost worse than having no power, he had more self-confidence than anyone else in our class. In a way I sort of envied him . . . at least when he wasn't annoying the living daylights out of me.

"Oh, nothing," Plasma Girl said. "We were just discussing the AI Collector Card series."

"Aren't they amathing!" he spit. "I've already athembled forty-theven cards!"

"We've got all but one of them," Halogen Boy volunteered.

"Well, if you thtick to it, you thould be able to catth up," Melonhead responded, completely ignoring the fact that we were already way ahead of him. "Perthaveranthe, that'th my motto," he added as he took his seat in front of Tadpole.

"Don't think about it," Plasma Girl said to Halogen Boy, who was racking his brain to figure out how Melonhead could be doing better than us. "We still need only one card."

"Yeah," agreed Tadpole. "We just have to go out and look for it."

"You're partly right," I finally spoke up. "We will keep looking. But I also happen to know what we're looking for!"

"You do?" Halogen Boy said. He lit up with excitement.

"Of course he does," said Plasma Girl, not even looking up as she blew on her nails to dry them. "Go ahead and tell us, O Boy."

First I told them what I had learned about Meteor Boy. They were all as surprised as I had been.

"Wow! That would be so cool, fighting alongside AI," Halogen Boy said dreamily.

"Are you nuts?" said Tadpole. "Didn't you hear what happened to Meteor Boy?"

I was a little annoyed at Tadpole for snapping at Hal. It isn't Hal's fault that he's a little slow. He just needed a moment to think about it and, sure enough, his excitement, as well as his glow, faded noticeably.

"So, anyway," I pushed on, "that leaves us with thirty-two cards of AI, sixteen cards of other heroes—but only fifteen cards with villains. Clearly the missing card is a villain."

"It makes sense," Plasma Girl agreed. "But who?"

"Think about it," I said. "Who is AI's first and greatest foe? Who destroyed Meteor Boy? Who is constantly setting up AI's most difficult challenges—at least on TV, anyway? And who is nowhere to be seen among the sixty-three cards we already have?"

"Professor Brain-Drain!" all four of them said in unison.

"Exactly!" I said.

"What's that about Professor Brain-Drain?" came a voice from the front of the class.

Our teacher, Miss Marble, had come into the room. Her hands were folded over her ample midsection as one foot tapped in irritation.

"Uh-um," I stuttered for a moment. "We were just talking about the Professor Brain-Drain card that we're missing from our set of Amazing Indestructo Collector Cards." I blurted out the truth in that frustrating way you do when you can't think of a good fib fast enough.

"Well, as long as it's something important," Miss Marble said in a tone that clearly indicated she didn't think it was important at all. "How many of the rest of you are also attempting to collect these cards?"

The hand of every kid in the class shot up. I felt vindicated! But then they all immediately began talking to each other.

"Did you see the card with my uncle on it?" Cannonball announced to anyone who would listen.

His uncle was the Crimson Creampuff, and Cannonball was incredibly proud to have a relative in the League of Ultimate Goodness. Whenever I felt jealous, I reminded myself that the Crimson Creampuff was one of the *least* competent members of the League.

"I'm missing twenty-three cards, including Whistlin' Dixie, the Animator, and Moleman," said Transparent Girl, from what looked like an empty seat on Hal's left. "If anyone has them, I'd be happy to hold onto them for you."

Even with our hands still raised, everyone began chattering, comparing notes on how their various collections were coming. No one was paying attention to Miss Marble any longer, which is never a good thing. Sure enough, I felt the inevitable reach of her power begin as a tingle in my left leg. Not wanting my hand to get stuck in the air, I quickly lowered my arm only a moment before I found myself frozen in a state of suspended animation.

Miss Marble got her name from her ability to freeze a person in place just as if he were a marble statue. The suspension never lasted more than a couple of minutes, but it made for a handy way to get the attention of . . . well, in this case, a class full of disruptive students.

"Now that I've frozen your mouths shut, let's have a little discussion about something called scarcity." Miss Marble glanced around the room at her students, who were petrified in poses ranging from acrobatic to downright uncomfortable. "Do any of you know what that word means?"

I knew what the word meant, but there was no way to put my hand back up or to even speak, for that matter.

"What's the matter, kids? Cat got your tongues? Ha-ha-ha-ha!"

Miss Marble often said the exact same thing after freezing us, and always laughed hysterically at her own bad joke. Of course, we all just sat there, stiff as boards. The feeling began to pass after a few minutes, and soon I was able to move my eyelids. As movement returned to the rest of the class, kids lowered their tired arms and remained quietly in their seats. No one ever wanted to risk a second freezing right away.

"So, scarcity. How about you, Hal?" Miss Marble continued, nodding at Halogen Boy.

Hal looked about helplessly. He can glow as brilliantly as an X-ray machine, but the sad fact is that he really isn't all that bright.

"Uh, I don't know," he said, before deciding to wing it, which for Halogen Boy is never a good idea. "Is it a city that's really scary?"

Miss Marble's eyes rolled to the back of her head. "No, it is not. Puddle Boy, do you know?"

Puddle Boy just nervously shook his head without saying a word. The puddle beneath his desk grew by another inch.

"How about you, Melonhead?"

"Thkarthity?" he said. Seeds splattered from his mouth in a dozen different directions. "Doethn't it mean generothity? Ath in "Thkarthity beginth at home?"

"Okay, Ordinary Boy," Miss Marble said, resignedly. "What does scarcity mean?"

It annoys me that she always assumes I know the answer. Well, okay, so most of the time I do. She still didn't need to pick on me.

"Scarcity is a term that refers to how difficult

something is to find," I said. "The fewer there are of an item that lots of people want, the more *scarce* that item is."

"Correct as usual," she said.

"Miss Marble?"

"Yes, Transparent Girl?" Miss Marble asked with a sigh of resignation.

"Scarcity is a term that refers to how difficult an item is to find," she pointed out perkily.

Miss Marble ignored her and pressed ahead. "Now tell me again, Ordinary Boy, what card haven't you been able to find?"

"I suspect that it's a card with Professor Brain-Drain on it," I answered.

"Has anyone found this card?" she asked the class as a whole.

Not a single hand was raised.

"It appears," she said directly to me, "that this card is *very* scarce, assuming that it exists at all. If it doesn't exist, you will all end up on a wild-goose chase and will no doubt spend much of your parents' money in the process."

"But what if it does exist?" I asked hopefully.

"Then," she answered, "if you find one, you will have found something that is very valuable indeed."

CHAPTER EIGHT

Straight to the Top

It was three o'clock and school had just let out. All five of us Junior Leaguers had agreed to meet at the end of the day to plan a strategy. We were waiting for Stench, who as usual needed to use the bathroom right after class.

While we waited, a large crate came floating up the sidewalk toward the school. It was only as it got closer that I saw it was being pushed along by an old friend of my dad's, and a former member of the New Crusaders, the Levitator.

"Hey, Lev," I waved. "How's it going?"

"Ordinary Boy!" he said in surprise as he poked his head around the crate. "Good to see you. How are your mom and dad doing?"

"They're great," I said, and then corrected myself.

"Well, my mom is doing fine. Dad's having a hard time getting back into crime fighting."

"Aren't we all." The Levitator laughed cheerfully. Even when he was down, he was still up—if you know what I mean. "It seems that all I can do for AI is deliver his products."

"What is this?" I asked, pointing at the enormous crate.

"It's a new vending machine for your lunchroom—courtesy of Indestructo Industries. Not that they won't make a nice profit in the process," he added. "It should be all set up for you kids by tomorrow. Take care!"

As the Levitator made his way toward the school, Stench charged up to us with a determined look on his face.

"We've got to find one of those cards," Stench blurted out as he reached us. "For three very good reasons: A) because it's valuable; B) because it completes our collection; and C) because it will really tick Miss Marble off."

"Yeah, did you see how she was practically daring us?" Tadpole fumed. "But we're not even completely certain what we're looking for."

"You heard O Boy," Plasma Girl said. "He's sure the card is of Professor Brain-Drain. Aren't you, O Boy?"

"I am," I said, and it occurred to me there was a way to confirm it. "And I have an idea. But it means we'll have to split up."

"Whatever you say, O Boy," Halogen Boy volunteered.

"Well, first, we should keep checking the card packs in the stores around the city," I said. "Tadpole, you and Hal go check out the Cavalcade of Candy. They should have lots for you to sort through. In the meantime, Stench, Plasma Girl, and I are going to go right to the source."

"You don't mean—" Plasma Girl started to say.

"Exactly," I confirmed. "The three of us are going to pay a call on Indestructo Industries. If anyone has an answer, it will be them."

We split into two groups and Tadpole and Halogen Boy headed in the direction of downtown. As Stench and Plasma Girl looked over my shoulder, I pulled out the *Li'l Hero's Handbook* and looked up Indestructo Industries in the "Places" directory.

With the address in hand, we headed off to the outskirts of town. It didn't surprise us that Indestructo Industries was one of Superopolis's most successful companies. We certainly bought enough of their products! But when we reached the address listed in the handbook, we couldn't believe the sleek, shiny office tower that awaited us. As we walked up the main sidewalk leading to the building, we passed under the legs

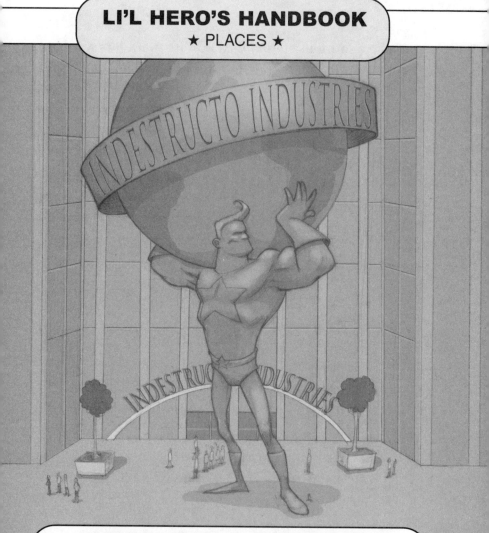

INDESTRUCTO INDUSTRIES

Located at 777 Indestructo Boulevard in the heart of the Indestructo Industrial Park, Indestructo Industries oversees all entertainment, merchandising, marketing, manufacturing and licensing operations for Superopolis's most financially successful hero, the Amazing Indestructo, as well as the League of Ultimate Goodness.

of the enormous statue of AI. On its shoulders was balanced a huge globe bearing the name of the company. It was impressive, but not more than I would expect for the greatest hero in Superopolis.

In the lobby we saw a directory, and we quickly found what we were looking for: Office of the President, twentieth floor. It made sense that the president would be at the top.

INDESTRUCTO INDUSTRIES

20th floor • Office of the President

19th floor • The Sentinels of Trademark Infringement

18th floor • The Defenders of Lawsuits

17th floor • The Federation of Fine Print

16th floor • The Syndicate of Shell Corporations

15th floor • The Human Resources Self-Preservation Squad

14th floor • The Enforcers of Corporate Euphemisms

13th floor • The League of Licensing, Royalties, & Copyrights

12th floor • The Proprietary Protectors of Patents

11th floor • The Association for the Exploitation of Adjectives

10th floor • The Union for Foodlike Substances

9th floor • Cafeteria/The League of Ultimate Goodness World Headquarters

8th floor • The Product Development Force

7th floor • The Secret Society of Safety Testers

6th floor • The Toxic Substance Recategorization Team

5th floor • The Choking Hazard Clearance Guild

"I'm not so sure we should be doing this." Plasma Girl stopped suddenly. "We could get into a lot of trouble and maybe even get yelled at."

As usual, Plasma Girl was thinking sensibly—the last thing a superhero on a mission wants to do. After all, if heroes thought sensibly, they'd stay home where it's safe. I was about to start my usual pep talk when we heard a raspy voice behind us.

"You kids must be here for the test-marketing study we're conducting today."

We turned around, and to our complete surprise, there was the Bee Lady! She's older now (and a lot heavier) and can only get around in a motorized scooter, but when she was younger, she was the first female member of the League of Ultimate Goodness. Just as in her heyday, she still has a real beehive woven into her hairdo. The bees that live in the hive, and which she has the power to control, were buzzing all around her head. Her black-and-yellow-striped spandex costume looked like it was being stretched to the breaking point.

Plasma Girl has always idolized the Bee Lady. She immediately began to gush.

"Bee Lady," she said in short, excited breaths, "what an honor to meet you! You have done so much to pave the way for female heroes everywhere!"

"Thanks, sweetie," the Bee Lady replied without sounding like she meant it. "I'm headed out to the parking lot for a cigarette, but you kids go on up to the eighth floor and I'll be right back to start the test marketing."

As the Bee Lady chugged away on her scooter, I ushered my teammates into the elevator and hit the button for the twentieth floor. The car zoomed to the top.

"Can you believe I actually met the Bee Lady?" Plasma Girl said excitedly.

"She didn't seem very

heroic," Stench said. I agreed but kept quiet to avoid the glare that Plasma Girl was now giving Stench.

"Well, she's older now," Plasma Girl snapped. "We'll see what you look like in sixty years."

Before my mind could form an image of an elderly Stench, the elevator doors opened onto a very expensive-looking reception area. There was a woman sitting at a desk, looking like she was doing something to her nails. As we came closer, I realized she was touching the nails on one hand with the index finger of her other. As she did, her nails changed from one color to another. That appeared to be the extent of her power.

"That is so cool!" Plasma Girl blurted out, clearly more impressed by the receptionist's power than I was.

"Is there something I can help you with?" the nail lady said, clearly irritated that we had interrupted her important task.

"We'd like to see the president, please," I asked as politely as possible. I also flashed my best "adorable child" expression. Adults usually love that. But not her.

"It ain't gonna happen, kid," she said, cracking a wad of bubble gum. "There's only one way to meet the president, and that's to have an appointment."

"Could we make an appointment?" I asked hopefully. I didn't bother with the sweet expression this time.

"Let me see . . ." She pretended to ponder my request for about five seconds. "NO!"

I couldn't believe that the Amazing Indestructo, the paragon of all that's good and right in the world, would have such an unpleasant person working for him.

"Okay, Stench," I said. "Maybe you can convince her."

The receptionist looked at us suspiciously. Plasma Girl and I knew to hold our breaths, but Fingernail Woman, or whatever her name was, did not. As Stench's powerful stink reached her nostrils, we watched her turn pale and clutch her desk with her colorful fingertips. A second later she was on her feet and running through the door that led to the executive offices. I grabbed the door before it closed and motioned with my head for Plasma Girl and Stench to follow me. The door clicked shut behind us, and it was safe to breathe again.

"Okay," I said, "the annoying woman went to the left, so I say we head to the right."

We ran down the carpeted hallway, trying all the doors on each side in hope of finding the one that would lead us to the president of Indestructo Industries. Every door was locked. When we reached the end of the corridor, there was only one door left to try. I reached for the knob, and, to my surprise, it turned. But that was nothing compared to the surprise I got when I opened the door. Because standing there, right inside the doorway, was that epitome of all that is evil, Professor Brain-Drain himself.

CHAPTER NINE

Business Is Business

We all stood there frozen with terror as Professor Brain-Drain stared down at us. It was impossible to make out his expression behind the incredibly thick glasses he wore, but there was no mistaking who we were dealing with. He was dressed completely in black except for his white lab coat, and the colander on his head shone eerily beneath the fluorescent lighting. And then

something truly odd happened. The door swung open a little farther and I noticed that there was another Professor Brain-Drain standing behind him. I poked my head inside and to my utter astonishment saw dozens of Professor Brain-Drains. There were short Brain-Drains and tall Brain-Drains. There were fat ones and skinny ones. There were Brain-Drains with hair, and Brain-Drains with warts. There was even one Professor Brain-Drain that was a woman. Finally, a Brain-Drain with bushy red hair and a potato chip bowl on his head spoke up.

"Don't you kids think you're a little young to stand a chance?"

"Stand a chance of what?" I asked. "What's going on here?"

"The tryouts, of course," said a Brain-Drain dressed in black leather and sporting a handlebar mustache.

"There was an open casting call for the role of

Professor Brain-Drain for AI's television show," explained another Brain-Drain as he practiced his tap-dancing routine.

"We're all here to audition," added the woman who was dressed as Professor Brain-Drain.

"But Professor Brain-Drain is a man," Stench pointed out.

"That's just the kind of conventional thinking that will keep you a slave to society your entire life," she sniffed with disdain.

While Stench was trying to figure that one out, I decided it was time to get back to our original goal and began to back out of the room. I motioned to Plasma Girl and Stench to follow.

"Well, good luck to all of you," I said as we stepped back into the hallway. Then I grabbed the knob and pulled the door shut.

"That was really weird," Stench stated.

Neither Plasma Girl nor I disagreed. We figured the president's office had to be in the opposite direction, so that's where we headed. As we passed by the reception area, we saw that the Fingernail Woman had returned. She had found a can of deodorizer and was so busy spraying it about her work area that she didn't notice us.

A few seconds later we were standing at the door to

an office that proudly announced: PRESIDENT OF INDE-STRUCTO INDUSTRIES.

"Do you suppose he's inside?" asked Stench. "And who *is* the president anyway? Do you think it might be AI himself?"

Plasma Girl and I just shrugged.

"There's only one way to find out," I said, secretly thrilled at the prospect of possibly meeting the Amazing Indestructo face-to-face. I reached boldly for the doorknob—but the door was locked.

"Actually, there's another way," Plasma Girl corrected me.

Stench and I watched as Plasma Girl's purplish-pinkish-bluish costume began to bubble and foam. A second later she had metamorphosed into a gelatinous glob, collapsing into a puddle on the floor. The puddle began to move, sliding effortlessly underneath the locked door in front of us. Soon after that, we heard the lock click from within, and the door opened.

"Is anyone in here?" Stench asked as we entered the enormous office.

"Not that I can see," replied Plasma Girl as her skin stopped bubbling and she returned to her usual self.

The office seemed empty, but I was getting a creepy feeling that we weren't alone. I turned around quickly to see if anyone was standing behind us, but all

I saw was the empty corridor we had just passed through. Then I took a good look at the office.

"Wow! Look at all this cool stuff," I said as it sank in. Set up on display tables and shelves throughout the room were a complete range of Amazing Indestructo products. There was the AI SuperBaby Crib with bendable iron bars that I had when I was really little; the Professor Brain-Drain Punching Bag; a copy of the first issue of *The Amazing Indestructo (and the League of Ultimate Goodness)* comic book; and (holy criminy!) even a complete set of all eight of AI's Power Vehicles, including his Atomic-Powered Rickshaw! These had been offered as prizes inside kids' Dinky Meals at the Dinky Dogs fast-food chain. I had found all of them except the rickshaw. In fact, no one I know had ever found one. As my shaking hand reached for the rickshaw, a voice suddenly interrupted me.

"Please don't touch that. It's the only one in existence."

We all turned and saw a man who looked about fifty. He was seated in a chair that had been turned away from us when we had first come in but was now swung around to face us. The first thing I noticed about him was that he wasn't wearing a costume. I mean, he wasn't naked or anything like that. It's just that instead of tights and a cape, he was dressed in an ordinary suit and tie—actually, a very expensive-looking suit and tie. He also did not seem the least bit pleased to see us in his office.

"Are you the president of Indestructo Industries?" I asked.

"I am," he said coolly. "My name is the Tycoon. My power is making money—lots of it."

"I've never heard of you before," Plasma Girl spoke up.

"That's the way I like it. Now how did you get in here?" he asked. "And what's happened to my secretary?"

"She went to get some fresh air," I said nervously. Then I built up my courage. "And we're here to talk to you about the collector cards you've just released."

Without saying a word, the Tycoon pressed a bright red button on a panel next to his phone. He then returned his attention to us.

"I'll be happy to answer whatever questions you like," he said with an oily smile. "You have about three minutes before the security guards I've just summoned arrive to remove you, so I suggest you ask quickly."

Plasma Girl and Stench both looked nervous, but I decided to get right to the point.

"Did you create a card for Professor Brain-Drain?" I asked.

"Yes," he answered.

"Are they in packs that are available to buy in stores?"

"Of course," the Tycoon replied.

"How many are out there?" I pressed.

"Three," he said as the corners of his mouth turned up in an evil-looking smile.

"Three!?" Stench said in outrage. "No wonder we couldn't find one!"

"If I'd had my way," the Tycoon continued, "there wouldn't have been even that many. But we ran into a little trouble with the Superopolis Trade Commission when we ran our last Dinky Meal promotion. They were outraged when we advertised for kids to collect all eight of those toys that you were just admiring—especially since we only manufactured seven of them. They threatened to close us down if we ever did anything like that again."

"You creep," Stench said. "I must have eaten over a hundred of those meals trying to find the Atomic-Powered Rickshaw."

"It shows, kid," the Tycoon said. Stench turned red with anger. To be honest, Stench isn't fat at all. He's just big.

"But that was the plan," he continued. "We sold tons of those meals. Just like we'll sell tons of these

NAME: Tycoon, The. **POWER:** An unfailing ability to make money.
LIMITATIONS: Vulnerable to tax collectors. **CAREER:** President of
Indestructo Industries. **CLASSIFICATION:** Loaded.

card packs as you kids go crazy trying to find them all."

"The Amazing Indestructo would toss you in jail if he knew what you were up to," I accused the Tycoon.

"Oooh, well I'll guess I'll have to make sure he doesn't find out." The Tycoon laughed. "Come on. AI himself suggested that there be thirty-two cards of him, sixteen cards of the LUG's, and sixteen cards of his villains. He hates Professor Brain-Drain so much he won't exactly be disappointed that there aren't very many of him."

"Where are the three Professor Brain-Drain cards?" I demanded, figuring I might as well ask.

The Tycoon stared at me for a moment with a mildly amused expression on his face. "I admire your spunk, kid," he said finally. "But of course I won't tell you exactly. I will, however, give you a hint: Just look near the three types of rock."

I had no idea what he meant by that, but before I could say anything, six brawny guards burst into the office. As the two who came for me grabbed hold of my arms, I glanced over and saw Stench easily lifting his two into the air, one in each hand. Plasma Girl had morphed into a glob, and her two guards were frantically trying to get her into an Amazing Indestructo Slot Machine coin bucket that one of them had grabbed from a display table. As usual, I was useless,

98

and I soon found myself being dragged from the office.

"Wait a minute," I yelled to the Tycoon. "What about Meteor Boy? How did he get into the collection?"

"Interesting question," he replied. I heard a sizzle of electricity and noticed Stench slump. "As you know, there are ten current members of LUG, plus the five original members, now retired. I needed sixteen heroes. At first I was going to use the Weatherman, but he's gone solo now and wouldn't give me permission."

"And?" I insisted. I had been dragged to the door and was now clinging to its frame. Stench looked unconscious as the two guards attempted to lift and drag him through the door, and the final two guards had succeeded in trapping Plasma Girl in the bucket.

"And so I took it upon myself to use Meteor Boy on the sixteenth card. I doubt that AI will mind. After all, we only created ten copies of it. I'm impressed that you even found one."

That was the last I heard. The office door swung shut. As the two security guards hauled me away, I could have sworn that I saw a figure dart out the door before it closed. But a second later it was gone. Meanwhile, Stench, Plasma Girl, and I found ourselves being dragged toward the elevator.

CHAPTER TEN

A Rocky Start

I was thrown out the front door of Indestructo Industries and landed right beneath the enormous statue of the Amazing Indestructo. Stench came rolling behind me, his eyes finally blinking back open as he bumped into AI's enormous boot. The last of the security guards took the bucket and tossed its contents onto the sidewalk. A few moments later, the goop had reconstituted itself back into Plasma Girl.

"How rude," she said, sticking her tongue out at the departing guards.

"At least you didn't get shocked," Stench said as he tried shaking some life back into his left hand. "I think one of those guys must be able to generate an electrical charge or something."

"Well, I'll tell you one thing. I'm never going to

buy anything from this company again," she added. "Not even the new Bee Lady Girl-Power Tea Set complete with recipes for Honey Crumpets and Nectar-Ade." She paused for just a moment. "Even though I really, really wanted it."

Stench and I just looked at each other. Neither of us was ready to make such a drastic pledge. I couldn't help thinking, that Plasma Girl had a point. But right now we had to try and figure out where the three Professor Brain-Drain cards were.

"Come on," I said. "It's almost four o'clock. Let's go meet Tadpole and Hal. We can figure out later how to tell AI what the Tycoon is up to."

The Cavalcade of Candy was the biggest candy store in town. Shaped like a dollop of whipped cream, it was a hundred feet tall, but the entire interior was as hollow as a chocolate bunny. One long pathway inside the store spun its way to the top in a single continuous spiral.

All along this path were individual shops specializing in any type of candy you could possibly imagine: chocolates, toffees, brittles, cotton candy, licorice—you name it. Running all through the open space in the middle there was also an incredible roller coaster called the Sugar Rush. In my opinion, though, the coolest thing there was the scale model of Superopolis that

THE CAVALCADE OF CANDY

The brainchild of the Superopolis Dental League, the Cavalcade of
Candy was built on the same location as their previous enterprise, the
Little Tykes Puck-Whacker Hockey Arena, which had been shut down
by the city over its refusal to provide kids with face masks. Home to
nearly one hundred confectioners, the Cavalcade of Candy was a success from the day it opened and is recommended by four out of five
dentists.

covered the main floor and was made entirely of candy. Mountains were made out of chocolate, trees were made from wisps of green cotton candy, and the buildings were made of gingerbread. It was completely accurate, too. I could even find the model of my own house!

There was no time to spend looking at it now, though. Plasma Girl, Stench, and I headed up the spiral pathway. We passed the Rock Candy Menagerie, where they sold little figures of animals made of rock candy, scooted by Great Balls o' Fire, whose jalapeño fireballs are even too hot for my dad, skirted around the Gummy Grave Robber, who sold gummy candy that looked like most of the major internal organs (Plasma Girl made an ick face as we passed by), until finally we reached the Collector Card Coliseum.

The department is enormous, but it was easy for us to follow the flashes of light over to where Halogen Boy was lighting up packs of cards while Tadpole checked out their contents.

"Any luck?" I asked.

"None at all," Tadpole responded. "But we only just got started. Hal insisted on having a large Apple Super Seltzer at the Fizz Bar before we started looking, and the carbonation gave his light such an on-and-off flashy quality that I couldn't focus on anything in the packs. It was only after he went to the bathroom that he toned down enough to be useful."

Tadpole gave Hal an annoyed look, but he just shrugged his shoulders innocently and burped.

"There are hundreds of packs to look through, though," Tadpole added hopefully.

"To be honest, I don't think there's any point in even checking," I said, and then I told them what we had learned at Indestructo Industries.

"How are we going to find three cards scattered all across Superopolis?" Tadpole exclaimed in frustration.

"Our only chance is the clue that the Tycoon gave us," I said. "What could he have meant by three types of rock?"

"Maybe he meant rock music!" Plasma Girl blurted out hopefully. "Let's see, what are the different types?"

"There's Heavy Metal," Tadpole suggested.

"Right," Plasma Girl agreed. "And there's Punk Rock."

"What about Rap?" Hal added helpfully. "Is that a type of rock?"

"I'm not sure that even counts as music," Stench said.

I was only half listening. I drifted over to the railing where I glanced down at the scale model of Superopolis.

My eyes focused on an enormous chocolate mountain in the center of the model. That was all it took for me to realize we were completely on the wrong track.

"He wasn't talking about rock music," I said, interrupting a discussion about the difference between Light Rock and Soft Rock. "He was talking about *rocks*!"

"What do you mean?" Plasma Girl asked.

"I mean regular, ordinary, old everyday rocks. The kind you find on the ground."

"That doesn't make any sense," Tadpole said. "There are millions of different rocks."

"No," I corrected him, "there are only three. Don't you remember in science class when we learned the three types?"

They all looked at me blankly, indicating how little they had absorbed of Miss Marble's recent lessons on geology.

"I sort of remember a little about it," Plasma Girl offered. "Just not very much."

"Okay, fine," I said. "Let me refresh your memories. Rocks are divided into three types—igneous, sedimentary, and metamorphic."

The blank looks remained in place.

"Let's start with igneous," I said. "Igneous rocks are crystal or glassy types of rocks that are created by molten lava when it cools."

As they stood there silently, I realized I wasn't getting through to them. So I jumped ahead.

"What it means," I said triumphantly, "is that I know exactly where one of the cards is located."

CHAPTER ELEVEN

Lava's Labors Lost

In the heart of downtown Superopolis is Lava Park. It's called that because there is a live volcano smack in the middle of it. The volcano, Mount Reliable, erupts every day at exactly five o'clock. And without fail, one of Superopolis's many heroes arrives on the scene and prevents it from doing any damage.

"The best example of igneous rock in all Superopolis is in Lava Park," I informed my teammates. "Igneous rock comes from lava that has hardened. It makes perfect sense."

"But how do we find a card that's hidden in a live volcano?" Halogen Boy asked, glowing dimly.

"It's not in the volcano," I responded. "Can you think of a place that normally sells this sort of thing and also happens to be located right near the volcano?"

LAVA PARK

After early attempts to sell the land around Mount Reliable as housing lots failed, the city leaders gave up and declared the area a municipal park. At over two hundred acres, the park now provides a needed oasis of green (and bubbling red) in the heart of the Superopolis business district. The numerous thermal vents throughout the park make it particularly popular for barbecues.

"Inkblot's Newsstand!" Plasma Girl cried.

"Exactly!" I said.

The Inkblot has had his newsstand on a corner of Lava Park for over fifty years. In that time he's watched lots of major historical events pass by on the front pages of the newspapers he sells there. Today's headlines weren't all that earthshaking, though. *The Hero Herald* had a headline about an investigation into the unusually large number of solid gold thimbles that Mayor Whitewash recently received as gifts—" They're only thimbles of appreciation" the headline quoted the mayor as saying. *The Weekly Daily* had a story about the enormous jackpot available in the Superopolis Lottery, which of course was pointless since the drawing had already happened three days ago, and *The Superopolis Times* had a piece on AI's capture of the Multiplier. They reported the Multiplier's dramatic increase in power, but there was no mention of the fact that my dad and the Big Bouncer had really brought him down.

In addition to papers and magazines, the Inkblot's stand also has a wide array of snack-size bags of potato chips, a selection of candy bars and breath mints, and, sure enough, a small assortment of card packs. Among them was a stack of Amazing Indestructo Collector Cards.

"Hello, young uns," the Inkblot greeted us as we made straight for the cards. "Can't get enough of that AI stuff, can you? When I was just a sprout, I was the same way about Captain Radio. You kids probably don't remember him, but he was the Amazing Indestructo of his day. He could ride the radio waves like one o' them surfer dudes. Now that was a power! I still remember the day I met him. I must have been about the age you whippersnappers are now. I couldn't wait to show him my power."

Hal illuminated his hand and I tried to both check out the cards and look like I was listening politely.

"I was still young enough to think my power was pretty impressive," the Inkblot continued. "I was in my brand-new costume. White as snow it was, except for the shape of a dark blot of ink smack in the middle of my chest. My boots, belt, and cape were the same dark color as the blot. I felt like I could take on every villain in Superopolis! That's when I met the captain."

We were halfway through the cards at this point, but there was no sign of a Professor Brain-Drain card. The Inkblot kept rambling on, now seemingly telling his story to a pigeon that had landed on the far edge of his counter.

"'Well, sir,' I said to him, 'wait' 'til you see this!' Then I took out my bottle of ink and poured it into my hand. Of course, it didn't land there, ya see, because that's my power. I can repel ink from my body, ya know! So I held out my hand to Captain Radio and the blob of ink hovered in the air above my palm. I moved that blob from hand to hand, working up its speed, and then, *wham!* I sent that inkblot flying through the air until it went *splat* against a wall over ten feet away."

I only heard a portion of this. We were down to the last couple of packs, and there was still no sign of the card.

"I turned to the captain," the Inkblot continued, "sure that he would be as impressed with my power as I was. He stood there silently for a few moments as my heart beat with excitement. I figured my skill had left him speechless. Then he burst out laughing, hopped onto a radio wave, and surfed away without saying a word to me. I felt pretty lousy for a while, but I also grew up a little that day. It wasn't long after that I got my first job selling newspapers. And in sixty years, I haven't once gotten my hands dirty handling them."

The Inkblot finished his story and held out his ink-free hands for me to inspect. We had gone through all the packs, and none of them contained a Professor Brain-Drain card. Before I could ask him about it, though, an enormous rumble suddenly threw us all to the ground. Mount Reliable began to spit balls of fire into the sky. Tadpole shouted, "Hey, guys, look! It's the Weatherman!"

Sure enough, the Weatherman himself was taking on today's volcano duty. Soaring to the top of the peak, he whipped up a blizzard over the mouth of the volcano, instantly freezing the lava that erupted into the air. For five minutes he kept at it, turning molten lava into—well, igneous rock. Finally, right on schedule, the volcano calmed down. After waving to the cheering crowd that had stopped to watch his performance, the Weatherman glided off on an air current into the late afternoon sky.

"I could save Superopolis, too," the Inkblot grumbled, "if the consarned thing ever erupted in ink."

This brought me back to the issue at hand.

"Inkblot, are these all the cards that you have?" I asked, trying not to sound desperate.

"Sure are," he replied. "I just put 'em out about an hour ago. Only sold one other pack, so far."

We all looked at each other in despair. Could it have been the one with our card?

"In fact," the Inkblot continued, "there's the little tyke that I sold it to, right over there."

He pointed to a kid who couldn't have been much older than four. He was standing near a park bench with his mother and was just opening a pack of cards.

We all gasped as we saw him reveal first one card with AI on it and then a second that clearly showed Professor Brain-Drain himself. The little kid snarled.

"Professor Brain-Drain?" he growled. "I hate Professor Brain-Drain. He's evil!"

Then, as we stood there helplessly, the kid took the card, crumpled it up, and tossed it into his mouth. That's when we noticed that his teeth were all sharp points of metal. It only took a couple of chews before he spit the completely ground-up card onto the sidewalk.

One Professor Brain-Drain card destroyed—only two left in all Superopolis.

CHAPTER TWELVE

The Anthill of Terror

We all stood looking down at the chewed-up remains of one of the only three Professor Brain-Drain collector cards in existence. The little monster who had left it in this state was now strolling away with his mother. As I stared after him, I thought I saw a shadowy figure moving in the trees nearby. But then I blinked, and it was gone.

"We were so close!" wailed Tadpole.

"But at least it proves that O Boy's theory is correct," Plasma Girl added, trying to sound optimistic. "Now we just have to figure out where the next one is and get to it first."

"Do you know where it is, O Boy?" Hal asked hopefully.

"Well, I've been thinking about the second type of rock, sedimentary," I said. "You guys all remember what sedimentary rock is, right?"

"Um, sure," said Stench. "But go ahead and remind us anyway."

The rest of the gang nodded.

"Right," I said, even though I could tell they had no idea. "Sedimentary rock is made up of small particles that accumulate over long periods of time. As weight presses them down, these particles, or sediment, fuse together and become rock. So the next location to check is obvious."

"It is?" said Hal.

"Of course," I replied. "We can't get at the sedimentary rock that is buried under layers and layers of earth, but it always has to start out as a top layer at some point."

"I'm not sure I'm following you," said Stench.

"Let me give you one more hint. One of the most common types of sedimentary rock is sandstone."

"The beach!" said Plasma Girl.

"Right," I replied. "The sedimentary rock of the future exists right now in the form of sand all over MegaManly Beach."

"There's only one place at the beach that might have AI Collector Cards," said Plasma Girl, "and that's Aunty Penny's Arcade."

A boardwalk separates downtown from the beach,

and there's an entire strip of cool shops set up along it. The one we were heading for was Aunty Penny's Arcade. You could get all sorts of neat things there. But you couldn't buy them—you had to win them. There were dozens of different games to play to win tickets, which you could exchange for incredible prizes. Well, okay, most of the prizes were pretty chintzy. But who cares! The fun was in winning them.

The first thing we saw as we entered the arcade was the huge sign that said: THE USE OF SUPER POWERS IS STRICTLY PROHIBITED. That's what I always liked about this place. Everyone else was on an equal level with me. In fact, I usually had an advantage, because most people in Superopolis are helpless when they can't use their powers.

The second thing I noticed was the box of Amazing Indestructo Collector Card packs that was sitting smack at the front of the prize display case. I went up to the counter to talk to Fly Guy, the manager of Aunty Penny's Arcade. Of course, he isn't actually a fly. In fact he looks completely human— except for his eyes. They bulge out from his head, and each one has dozens of facets that allow him to see what is going on all over the place. He also sort of buzzes when he talks, but he only does that to scare

the littler kids into thinking he really is a fly.

"How long have you had these available?" I asked, pointing at the cards.

"I just put 'em out today, kidzzz," he buzzed. "Only thirteen prizzze tickets will get you a pack."

"How many packs are there total?"

"Thirty-six," he answered. "You could be the first to claim them azzz a prizzze."

"Fantastic!" I said. "We're going to win every one of them!"

"Just make sure you don't use any superpowerzzz," he added suspiciously, "or I'll toss you out of here on your buttzzz."

I couldn't help but smile. "Oh, there won't be any danger of that."

I returned to where the rest of the team was waiting and explained to them that we could get a pack for every thirteen tickets we won. Unfortunately, if the right pack was the last one in the box, it would ultimately require 468 tickets to get it.

"It stinks that we can't just sneak a look at them and find the one we need," Stench said.

"That's not all that stinks," added Plasma Girl, as she, Tadpole, and Hal began backing away from Stench.

"Sorry." He shrugged, reaching for one of his

canisters of deodorizer. "That happens sometimes when I get upset."

"Unfortunately, we can't get a look at them unless we win them," I explained. "Why don't you go over to the Anthill of Terror, Stench, since you're always good at that. And we'll go try some of the games over here."

"Yeah, yeah. I can take a hint," Stench grumbled. Turning, he stalked off in the opposite direction, fuming in more ways than one.

From a safe distance, I kept one eye on Stench as he wandered over to where an anthill rose about five feet off the floor. It had a three-foot-high plastic wall surrounding it and scary-looking neon letters mounted above that proclaimed: THE ANTHILL OF TERROR!

Stench picked up a fishing pole that had a magnet swinging at the end of its line. He dropped a quarter into a coin slot next to the game. The anthill immediately started rumbling. A few seconds later dozens and dozens of plastic ants began pouring out of the top and sliding down the sides. The ants were made out of plastic, but some of them also had a metal ball bearing inside. These were the ones that Stench was after. He swung his line over the plastic wall smack into a pile of the churning critters, then reeled it back in with one of the ants sticking to the magnet.

Lifting it over the wall, he removed the ant and

quickly recast his line. Ants were still pouring from the hill, but they were also disappearing into a channel in the base. His second cast landed in the biggest pile of the tumbling "terror" ants. But each time he raised his line there was nothing attached to it. After two attempts, he only captured one more ant.

The number of ants now coming out of the top began to dwindle. Stench had never gotten fewer than five ants. He threw his line once again into a mass of the seething insects, and once again came up empty. The ants had now stopped emerging, and the ones that were still visible were quickly reaching the base and vanishing. In a last desperate act, he swung his line over one of the last remaining ants and it rose up and attached itself to the magnet.

"What's the deal with the Anthill of Terror?" I heard Stench gripe to Fly Guy. "I've always gotten at least five."

"That wazzz the problem, kid," he buzzed. "Everyone else did, too. So I took out half the ball bearingzzz."

"Does Aunty Penny know you're giving her a bad name?" Stench asked.

"It wazzz her idea. She needzzz the money to pay for her new nozzze job."

"That reeks," Stench mumbled to himself as he dropped his ants into a box alongside the anthill. It spit

out three tickets in exchange. "At this rate it will take forever to get the four hundred and sixty-eight tickets we need." Not to mention cost a fortune in the process, I thought.

CHAPTER THIRTEEN

Winner Takes None

It was a frustrated and irritated Stench who made his way back to where Tadpole and I were playing Bonk the Squirrels.

"Did you see how I got robbed?" he asked me. "I only managed to get three tickets off the Anthill of Terror."

"That stinks," Tadpole said. Cautiously, he sniffed the air to make sure nothing else stank. Then, winding up his arm, he pitched the large plastic acorn in his fist at a small circular opening. Inside was a flat metal plate that was painted to look like a taunting squirrel. The acorn hit the squirrel smack in the chest, knocking it flat on its back, and five tickets were spit out of a slot right next to where Tadpole was standing.

"Excellent," Stench said as the flattened squirrel

sprang back up. "How many tickets do you have so far?"

"Only ten," Tadpole answered sadly. "That was my first five-pointer. The others have all been for only one or two tickets. O Boy's doing better."

He was right but only by a little. I had twelve tickets so far. Bonk the Squirrels was usually my best game, but not today. The game consists of a large wall with a tree painted on it and lots of openings cut into the bushy part. Within each circle is a squirrel. Some of the circles are large, making the squirrels easy to hit. The only problem is you don't get many tickets for hitting those. The circles get smaller as you go higher up the tree. They're harder to hit, but you can get a lot more points. Of course, up at the top is the smallest circle of all. It's worth five hundred tickets. Nobody's ever managed to knock over that squirrel, though.

"I can usually do better," I explained as I put in a quarter and got three more plastic acorns to throw, "but they don't seem to be falling over as easily as they used to."

"Fly Guy probably tightened the springs," Stench suggested, "just like he removed half the ball bearings in the Anthill of Terror."

I pitched an acorn straight at a squirrel that was worth ten points. It came incredibly close but caught

the edge of the opening and ricocheted off to the side.

"We're never going to get what we need at this rate," I said in frustration, "unless one of us can hit the five-hundred pointer."

"Give it a shot." Tadpole shrugged. "You might actually get it."

What the heck, I decided. I concentrated as hard as I could and wound up my pitch. With my eye glued to the spot, I threw the acorn, and it went sailing up toward its mark. To the complete surprise of all of us, it slipped perfectly through the tiny opening and hit the squirrel head-on.

"You hit it!" Tadpole and Stench both said in amazement.

But the squirrel didn't fall backward. As the acorn dropped away, the squirrel remained standing, its big buck teeth sticking out from its mocking grin.

"You totally had it, O Boy!" Tadpole complained. "What a rip-off."

"I'm beginning to think this whole place is a rip-off," Stench added, glancing accusingly over toward Fly Guy. He had his eyes all over us and a smirk on his face.

"You know what?" Tadpole whispered to us. "If there was a way to get all those eyes off us, I bet I could find out what's up with that squirrel."

"Good idea," I agreed. "Let's get Plasma Girl and

Hal. I may have a plan."

Plasma Girl was playing a round of Earthquake in Doll Land, but her character, Princess Patty-Cake, had just fallen into a crevice.

"I only managed to save two of the princess's unicorns before the royal stables collapsed," she said glumly, showing me the two tickets she had won.

"Don't worry about that for now," I said. "We're changing strategies. Let's get Hal."

We expected to find Hal at his favorite game, Toss the Cookies, but instead he'd found a new game we hadn't seen before at Aunty Penny's Arcade. It was called the Amazing Indestructo Retirement Fund Game and it had lights and buzzers all over it. The only instructions were on a sign that read: HELP THE AMAZING INDESTRUCTO FEND OFF AN INSOLVENT FUTURE! (Insert 25 cents). As we approached, Hal put in a quarter. All the lights and buzzers began to sound, but that was it. There were no controls and no way that I could see to win any tickets. It didn't take Hal long to confirm this.

"That's the sixth quarter I've put in this thing and I still haven't won any tickets," he said glumly.

I probably would have stopped after the second quarter, but I didn't say that to Hal. I looked down at the manufacturing plaque on the base of the machine and wasn't the least bit surprised to see that it was made by Indestructo Industries. As soon as our current mission was resolved, I was determined to let AI know what the Tycoon was doing to his good name.

"Don't worry about that now," I consoled Hal. "I've got a new plan. We need to create a diversion that will distract all the dozens of facets of Fly Guy's eyes. Stench, I want you to go over to the other side of the arcade and pretend to lose a quarter underneath the Hill o' Beans. Then start complaining as loudly as you can. When Fly Guy comes over to help Stench, that will be your sign, Hal."

"Sure, O Boy. Just tell me what to do."

"Run over and offer to provide some light. When you get there, illuminate yourself as brightly as possible. That will momentarily blind Fly Guy in all his eyes. Meanwhile, I'll let Tadpole know when it's safe for him to do his thing."

"What a great plan," Hal said as he brought his sippy cup to his lips and took a big gulp of apple juice. Then he and Stench moved off to take their positions.

When they were out of earshot, Plasma Girl turned to me.

"Is my job the usual one?" she asked, cocking an eyebrow.

"You got it," I replied. "Be ready to act as soon as Hal messes up his part of the plan."

"Roger." She saluted me and then turned to follow the other two.

Two minutes later, I heard Stench bellowing from across the arcade that he had lost his quarter. That was the only part of the plan that worked the way it was supposed to. Fly Guy immediately messed up everything by refusing to budge from his chair.

"Too bad, kid," I heard him say. "But thanks for the donation."

Unfortunately, Hal never thought to change his part of the plan and was soon running toward the Hill o' Beans. Thank goodness for Plasma Girl. She had turned herself into a pool of jelly on the floor right in Hal's path. Sure enough, he slipped on her and went sliding smack into the stack of bean cans that make up the Hill o' Beans. As they came crashing down around both him and Stench, it finally got Fly Guy to move.

"No powerzzz!" he buzzed angrily as he got up from his chair and ran toward the mess of bean cans.

Of course, he didn't notice Plasma Girl, either, so he, too, was soon sliding into the heap on the floor. Plasma Girl quickly returned to her normal shape.

"Hal," she shouted. "Lighten up."

Halogen Boy did as he was told, and soon the arcade was flooded with an intense light.

"Well, it wasn't exactly my plan," I said to Tadpole,

"but it'll do. Go ahead."

Tadpole shot out his tongue and it snaked its way up to the top cutout in the tree, slipping behind the stubborn squirrel. It didn't take Tadpole long to figure out the problem.

"He'th got a peg thtuck behind the thquirrel," he informed me. "There'th no way to knock the thing over."

"Can you remove it?" I asked him.

"Let me thee," he answered.

I glanced around to make sure that no one was watching. All of a sudden, I could have sworn I saw someone moving about behind the counter where the prizes were kept. At first I thought it must be Fly Guy. I squinted through the brightness at the chaos over by the Hill o' Beans. But Fly Guy was still there,

completely tangled in the mess. By the time I glanced back to the counter, whoever I had seen was gone. I didn't worry about it right then, though, because Tadpole yelled proudly, "I got it. The peg ith looth."

Wasting no time, he used his tongue to push the squirrel back onto its trigger and I soon heard five hundred tickets being spit out of the slot in front of me.

"We've got 'em," I told Tadpole as he put the peg back into place and pulled his tongue back into his mouth.

His timing was perfect. The second Hal's light began to fade, Fly Guy got up off the floor and most of his eyes were on us immediately. All he was able to see, however, was me folding up the wad of prize tickets. I took them straight over to the counter, but as I got there one thing was already clear—the box of card packs had been stolen.

CHAPTER FOURTEEN

Change Is Good

By the time we found ourselves being tossed out of the arcade, still clutching our five hundred prize tickets, it was nearly six o'clock, and we all had to be home for dinner. We agreed we would regroup tomorrow at school.

As I trudged up the sidewalk to my front door that evening, I felt frustrated and confused. First of all, who stole the box of card packs from Aunty Penny's Arcade? Three times today I thought I saw someone shadowing us. It had happened first at Indestructo Industries, again at Lava Park, and then again at the arcade. No one else had noticed anything, though, so I didn't tell the team.

Second, I was at a complete loss about the third type of rock, metamorphic. Then there was the problem of the Tycoon. The fact that he was out there blackening the good name of the Amazing Indestructo was an issue that would have to be dealt with.

Finally, I was feeling a little bit useless. After all, it had been my friends' powers that got us anywhere today. Stench and Plasma Girl had gotten us into Indestructo Industries. Tadpole had solved our squirrel problem. Even Halogen Boy, in his own hapless way, had somehow managed to make our diversion work at the arcade this afternoon.

All in all, I was pretty depressed by the time I came through the door.

"You're just in time, OB," my mom called from the kitchen. "Your father and I are setting out dinner."

As I stepped into the kitchen I saw Dad holding a metal broiling pan in his hands. The steaks on top were nearly done grilling. To be honest, I'm not sure why we even have a stove in our kitchen. I don't think we've ever used it.

"Oh, my. You look so sad," my mother said as soon as she saw me. "What's the matter, dear?"

I paused for a second, not sure how to answer that question. Suddenly, I couldn't help it. It all came pouring out.

"The Junior Leaguers have spent all day trying to

find the Professor Brain-Drain card, which is the only one we need to complete our AI Collector set, but we found out from this creep called the Tycoon who's messing up AI's reputation with all the bad things he's doing in his name that they only made three of them and spread them all over Superopolis in places that have to do with the three types of rock, and we were able to find the card linked with igneous rocks, but this stupid kid ate it, and we found the one that had to do with sedimentary rock, but some creep who I think was following us stole it before we could get it, and now I don't have a clue what location metamorphic rock might be referring to and why does it even matter since I don't have any superpower anyway!"

At least I didn't start crying. . . .

All right. So I did start crying. Not very much or very long, mind you . . . but enough that I couldn't pretend I only had something in my eye.

"OB." Mom knelt down in front of me, touching my tears with her fingertip. "Everything will be okay."

Each of my tears fell to the floor as a small crystal of ice. As I wrapped my arms around my mom and hugged her, Dad knelt down alongside us.

"Don't get down, hero," he said. "Let's just go over what happened today and we'll all put our noggins together and help you solve this."

I told them every-
thing as we sat down to
our dinner of steak and
chips. We were having Dr.
Telomere's Garlic-and-Onion-
flavored chips and they went
great with the steak. Oh,
yeah, there was a salad, too,
since Mom always insists that
we have some sort of veg-
etable. Dad and I would have
skipped that part if we could.

When I got to the part
about the third type of rock,
metamorphic, I was hoping
they might have
some ideas. Well,
they had some
ideas, all right.
They just weren't "good" ideas.

"Honey, what do you know about metamorphic
rock?" Mom asked Dad.

He sat there sort of blankly for a moment before he
responded. "Well," he said tentatively, "I used to know
a hero named the Metamorph."

Both Mom and I nodded expectantly.

"But he changed himself into a cockroach and someone stepped on him."

"Well, that's not very helpful," my mother said, speaking for both of us. "But the word *metamorphic* does refer to change."

My mom is a lot smarter than she lets on.

"That's true," I said. "Metamorphic rock is basically rock that was originally either igneous or sedimentary but changed because of conditions like high pressure or heat."

"I can show you heat!" my dad said in his booming voice, holding up his fork. Within seconds the metal fork melted and began to drip from his hand. Mom and I both watched politely.

"Do you know what the most common type of metamorphic rock is, OB?" my mother asked, turning back to me.

"I think it's slate," I answered.

"I think you're right," my mom said as she gave me a big smile. "And I don't think there are many heroes in this city who could have answered that question."

We both glanced over at my dad, who was wiping the last few molten drops of his fork onto his costume, while using his other hand to stuff a bunch of potato chips into his mouth.

"What?" he mumbled innocently.

"There's just one problem," I said. "I'm not sure where the clue is telling me to go."

"You've got all night to think about it," she said as she got up to start clearing the table. "And if anyone can figure it out, I know it's you."

Later that night, at bedtime, Dad came to tuck me in.

"Figured it out yet, OB?" he asked me as he pulled the bed covers up to my chin.

"Not yet. I haven't been able to make any kind of connection."

It was true. Ever since dinner, I'd been trying to first think of places that I knew would be selling the cards, and then figure out if those places had any possible connection to slate.

"You will," he said confidently.

Dad and Mom had so much faith in me. And I had been so busy with my problems that I hadn't bothered to ask either of them about their day.

"How is your hunt for a new team going, Dad?"

I could tell that he was happy I'd asked. But clearly things had not been going well for him either.

"Well, nothing is going to happen with the League of Ultimate Goodness. I'm about ready to give up and go back to the potato chip factory." He sighed as he lowered himself onto the edge of my bed and absentmindedly picked up the teddy bear that was sitting there. "I met with three other groups today and they all rejected me for being too old. Too old!" he repeated incredulously.

Then the best idea ever hit me.

"Dad, you're too good to be part of any of those teams," I blurted out.

"What do you suggest?" my dad asked.

"Put together your own team."

My father looked blank. I could see that the gears were turning, though. My eyes darted to my poor teddy bear, trapped in my father's unwitting grip.

"There's you, the Big Bouncer, the Levitator," I listed them off. "You all have cool powers, and I'll bet you know other really old guys who would like to fight crime again."

"They never said I was *really* old," he corrected me. "Just old."

"Your experience is worth more than all those other teams put together. Take advantage of it, and show Superopolis what you're capable of!"

"You're right!" he shouted as he leaped to his feet, raising my teddy bear triumphantly into the air with one hand. "I'll do it!"

My doomed teddy bear erupted in flames. Dad quickly dropped it and smothered it with his cape. It's frankly amazing that our house has never burned down.

At any rate, I couldn't have been happier about the change in my dad's mood.

"This is just what I need." My dad laughed. "It's time to wipe the slate clean and start over."

The words were barely out of Dad's mouth when the answer hit me. I knew exactly where to find the final Professor Brain-Drain card!

CHAPTER FIFTEEN

The Third Card

The next day, I got to school late and made it into the classroom just as the first bell rang. I was dying to tell the team what I had figured out, but there was no way to get the attention of all of them together.

Halogen Boy was busy fending off Transparent Girl's offers to trade her string of paper clips for our Meteor Boy card. Stench was shaking his head and rolling his eyes as Cannonball argued that the Crimson Creampuff was the second most powerful member of the League of Ultimate Goodness, right after AI himself. And Plasma Girl was deep in conversation with Little Miss Bubbles, who was showing off her new Whistlin' Dixie rhinestone bracelet with genuine imitation rhinestones. I could tell from the look on Plasma Girl's face that her pledge to contribute no more money to any business run by the Tycoon was already crumbling like a potato chip.

Meanwhile, Tadpole was having another of his pointless arguments with Melonhead.

"Listen, seed brain," Tadpole was saying, "if you tried using a rocket pack like AI's you'd burn your butt to a crisp the second you turned the thing on."

"I dithagree with your athethment," countered Melonhead. "The Amathing Indethructo manageth to avoid thcorching hith backthide."

"That's because he's indethructible—I mean, indestructible," Tadpole erupted in frustration.

I don't know why he bothers to argue with Melonhead. It's just part of his personality, I guess. There's nothing that Tadpole wouldn't do for a friend, but he has the shortest fuse of anyone I've ever met. He's also the most stubborn person I know. I could tell he was about to plunge back into the argument, but just then Miss Marble came into the room.

"Good morning, urchins," she said. She was in a surprisingly good mood for her. "Would any of you like to buy a Professor Brain-Drain card?"

I got an instant knot of despair in my gut as the hand of every kid in the class shot up in a chorus of "me, me, me's!" Had Miss Marble beaten us to the last Professor Brain-Drain card.

NAME: Tadpole. **POWER:** A fully manipulatible tongue that can stretch to nearly twenty feet. **LIMITATIONS:** About twenty feet. **CAREER:** Efforts to stretch his age have led to two attempts to join the League of Ultimate Goodness before turning ten; currently a member of the Junior Leaguers. **CLASSIFICATION:** A mouthy little son of a gun.

"Well, I wish I had one to sell you." She started laughing, enjoying the disappointed looks on everyone's faces. She can be a little nasty sometimes. Secretly, I was pretty relieved, though.

"I'm guessing that none of you are ready to give up on this quest yet, are you?" she continued. "May I ask how much money that could otherwise be going to fund your college educations is being wasted on this folly?"

"I've thpent theventy-theven dollarth tho far," Melonhead proclaimed proudly.

"I've used all the money I had been saving to buy a new bike," Lobster Boy piped up. "One hundred and ten dollars!"

"I only spent ninety-six dollars," admitted the Spore, with a wheezy gasp. "But that's because the store wouldn't take some of my money because of the mushrooms growing on it."

As all the kids in my class shouted out amounts of money, Miss Marble wrote them out on the chalkboard. I don't know if it was disgust over how much we had all spent, or possibly the realization that it added up to more than her annual salary, but I could tell her level of crankiness was growing. Sure enough, she spun around and hit us with the most powerful weapon at her disposal—a surprise assignment.

"That's enough," she said, interrupting Transparent Girl's attempt to top what everyone else had spent. "I want each of you to spend the remainder of the morning writing out an essay. The title will be: 'The Foolish Children Who Wasted All Their Money.' Begin now."

The morning crawled by as we all worked on our essays, but I finally got a chance to gather the team together at our pre-lunch recess.

While no one was looking I motioned them away from the playground and back into the school. Once inside, we headed to the hallway outside the cafeteria. There were only fifteen minutes left before lunch was going to start, so I got right to the point.

"I think it would be great to show everyone in class our new Professor Brain-Drain card right after lunch. Don't you guys?"

They all looked at me like I had a toilet plunger stuck on my head.

"Umm, O Boy. That would imply that we've actually *found* the Professor Brain-Drain card," Stench pointed out, "which, in fact, we have not."

"He's up to something," Plasma Girl said suspiciously as I stood there grinning. "What gives?"

"Did you find the third card after we split up?" Tadpole asked accusingly.

"No," I said, "but I did figure out where we'll find it."

"Where is it, O Boy?" Hal asked. This morning he had only a dim glow surrounding him.

"A place that has lots and lots of slate," I replied, "which just so happens to be the most common type of metamorphic rock."

"And where would that be?" Plasma Girl pushed, sounding irritated. I have to admit, I can be a little annoying when I know something that the others don't.

"Right here," I said.

"In the school?" Halogen Boy said.

"Exactly. A school with a slate blackboard in almost every room," I revealed. "In fact, there is more slate in this building than anywhere else in Superopolis."

"But there isn't any place in the school to buy the cards," an exasperated Plasma Girl blurted out.

I had thought the same thing at first, too. But then I remembered what we'd seen yesterday. I placed my hand on the door to the deserted cafeteria and flung it open.

"Isn't there?" I asked.

Straight ahead of us, glowing in the dimly lit room, sat the Amazing Indestructo Adventures in Vending machine. Since it had just been installed yesterday, I was sure we were the first to see it. At first glance it seemed to stock just the entire line of AI Candy Bars and Snack Cakes. I began to worry that I had been too cocky, but then I heard Plasma Girl gasp.

"Look, you guys!"

We all glanced up to where she was pointing, to the top row. Right next to AI's brand of dental floss (what were they thinking?) was a pack of Amazing Indestructo Collector Cards.

I took a dollar out of my pocket and fed it into the machine. Everyone held their breath as I punched in the

code number. It felt like an eternity as we heard the machine clank and grind, and then the pack of cards finally fell into the open slot. Reaching for it with a shaking hand, I picked it up and ripped it open. There staring back at us was a card with . . . who else? . . . the Amazing Indestructo.

We all groaned. Then I lifted it up to reveal behind it . . . the one and only remaining, genuine and original, Professor Brain-Drain card.

CHAPTER SIXTEEN

Homeroom Hysteria

Needless to say, everyone in our class that afternoon was incredibly jealous of us. We allowed the other kids to take a look at the Professor Brain-Drain card, but only from a safe distance. We didn't want someone like the Spore getting mold all over the thing or Melonhead spitting seeds on it.

Even Miss Marble was impressed. During our last class of the day we told her how we had learned about there being only three cards and how we had found them using the clue we'd been given.

"Very clever," she said. "And it would appear that you truly do have a very valuable item."

"That shows her," I heard Stench mumble under his breath.

"In fact," she continued, "let's try a little experiment

to see just how valuable it is. Okay, class. How many of you would like to own one of these tiny scraps of flimsy cardboard, printed with a penny's worth of ink to form an image of Professor Brain-Drain?"

Every hand in the class shot up. "Me, me, me!" they all shouted.

At this point Transparent Girl turned to me and offered me two dollars for the card, which, after all, she informed me, had only cost me a dollar. I told her to disappear completely and turned my attention back to Miss Marble.

"Tell me, Puddle Boy," Miss Marble said, "how much would you be willing to pay for a card like this?"

"I don't know. Maybe ten dollars?" he said hesitantly as a thin ripple spread across the pool beneath his desk.

"I'd pay twenty dollars," offered the Human Sponge. She turned to the Spore and asked him if she could borrow twenty dollars.

"Twenty dollarth?!" Melonhead said, spraying seeds everywhere. "I'd give thirty, pluth my entire thet of Thouth Theath thea thellth!"

"I'd trade fifty dollars and my bike," shouted Lobster Boy.

"The handlebars are all clawed up," accused Cannonball as everyone in the class began to shout.

"I'd give seventy-five dollars plus all my bowling trophies."

"I'd give my allowance for an entire year," the
Banshee suddenly screeched.

We all plugged our ears and ducked just in case one
of the windows shattered. Thankfully, the Banshee got
ahold of herself and the shrieking subsided quickly.

"I'd trade all thirty-two of my Amazing Indestructo
cards for just one Professor Brain-Drain card," shouted
Transparent Girl.

The fact that anyone could even utter such words
brought first a gasp and then a crushing silence to the
room.

"That's crazy!" gasped the Human Sponge as she finally absorbed what Transparent Girl had said.

Everyone was shocked. Such disloyalty to AI was unthinkable. Why, he was the greatest superhero in Superopolis, which surely made his cards more valuable than—

"I would, too," hollered Lobster Boy, breaking the tension.

"Tho would I," agreed Melonhead.

"Me, too." At least four other voices rang out in unison.

"I would trade them, too," the Banshee screeched yet again.

As we all covered our ears for a second time, Miss Marble finally acted, and I felt my entire body freeze. She started to speak, but none of us except the Banshee could hear what she had to say because we had all been frozen with our hands over our ears. By the time Miss Marble's power had worn off, everyone had finally calmed down.

"You've all just gotten a perfect example of the concept of scarcity," she said. "In this classroom alone I count seventeen kids besides you five who want this Professor Brain-Drain card, but only one exists. As a result, the amount that someone is willing to pay for it increases beyond its actual cost. In fact, the more people there are who want something rare, the higher the price of that item will rise. That is how the value of anything is determined."

"But this isn't the only card," I said, and immediately wished I hadn't. The entire class turned toward me like a pack of hungry animals. Unfortunately, I couldn't stop talking now, or they probably would have ripped me apart.

"One of the three cards is right here." I cautiously handed the card back to Stench. I knew he would be able to protect it. "Another one was destroyed at Lava Park. We think the last of the cards was at the arcade, but if it was, it was stolen before we confirmed it. But that means—"

"There'th thtill one card out there!" blurted Melonhead, seeds flying everywhere.

At exactly that moment, the bell rang. If anyone had been outside the classroom just then, he would have been trampled by seventeen stampeding junior heroes determined to find the last Professor Brain-Drain card. The five of us who already had one got up to leave as well, but much more calmly. Miss Marble watched us as we headed for the door.

"Be careful with that card," she said soberly as we filed past. "It could end up causing you an awful lot of trouble."

CHAPTER SEVENTEEN

TROUBLE INDEED

Keeping a close watch all around us, the gang and I headed straight for our headquarters. With something as valuable as what we were carrying, we needed to get it to safety as quickly as possible.

"Can you believe how crazy everyone is acting?" Plasma Girl said.

"Why wouldn't they?" Tadpole responded. "We have the most valuable object ever in the entire history of the known universe."

"I wouldn't say it's *that* valuable," I countered.

"Of course it is," said Stench. "You heard Miss Marble. She said it was worth a fortune."

"She also said it could cause us a lot of trouble," I pointed out. "So let's be careful with it."

As soon as we got to the tree house—I mean,

headquarters—we climbed up and pulled the ladder in behind us. Taking our usual seats on the couch and chairs, we set the card down on the table between us. All of us just stared at it for at least five minutes, not saying a word. Finally, Tadpole broke the silence.

"Do you think it will be safe here?" he said.

"Safe?" Stench said, clearly insulted. "Of course it will be safe. No one's ever gotten into this place that I didn't want to get in."

"You tell him, bro'."

We all spun around, and there was Stench's annoying older brother, Fuzz Boy. He must have come in before us and been hiding in the kitchen. I noticed that he was also now sporting a goatee that he must have created himself. As much as he'd like to think otherwise, he's not old enough to shave yet.

But he's definitely old enough to be irritating.

"How did you get in here?" Stench demanded as he got to his feet. "You know Dad said you're supposed to keep out."

"Take it easy, little whisker," Fuzz Boy said soothingly. "I was just hiding out here until I was certain Mom had gone. She was threatening to haul me in for a haircut."

"You really could use one, Fuzz Boy," I spoke up. "How do you even see with so much hair hanging in your eyes?"

"The name is just Fuzz," he said, pointing both index fingers at me and striking a pose that I think was supposed to look cool. "Drop the *Boy*, boy."

"Get out of here, or I'll drop you," Stench hollered, clenching his fist as he stepped right up to his brother.

"Chill out, little one," Fuzz Boy—er, excuse me, *Fuzz*—said as he swiftly stuck his finger under Stench's chin as if to tickle him. The touch was slight, but it was enough to cause a small clump of hair to grow out almost three inches. "You know what they say—hair today, gone tomorrow."

That was supposed to be the moment when Fuzz grabbed the rope ladder and made a smooth escape from the tree house. Unfortunately for him, he didn't realize we'd pulled the ladder in. There was nothing for him to grab, and he ended up plunging almost ten feet down to the lawn below, letting out a high-pitched, girly scream in the process. It wasn't exactly the graceful exit he had planned. Stench checked to see that he was okay, and then we all started laughing.

Unfortunately, Fuzz Boy's unwanted presence had revealed a flaw in our plan.

"Well, so much for our supersafe headquarters," Tadpole said snidely. "Now where do we put the card to protect it?"

"I could take it home and hide it inside some frilly outfit in my doll closet," Plasma Girl offered—quite sensibly, in my opinion.

"I should keep it at my house," Tadpole insisted loudly.

"It should stay with me," Stench insisted. "I'm the strongest one and I can protect it."

"No way, Stinky," Tadpole said, facing Stench belligerently. He had never been mad enough to call Stench by that name before.

"Stop fighting, you two," Plasma Girl interjected. "If anyone should take it home it's O Boy. He's the one who found it."

"Keep out of it," Tadpole and Stench turned to Plasma Girl and shouted simultaneously.

All three of them began screaming at one another.

I glanced over at Hal who was silently staring off into space. I knew how he hated to see any of us fighting. So did I. Miss Marble's final words to us were beginning to make an awful lot of sense. It was time for me to speak up.

"Everybody stop fighting," I hollered. I wasn't the Banshee, but I could yell when I had to.

There was an immediate silence, but before I could say anything, another voice spoke up.

"How about keeping it in the Hall of Trophies?" Halogen Boy suggested, indicating the upside-down aquarium. "It can go right next to our souvenir from the Mysterious Case of the Turning Doorknob."

All three of them looked at Hal like he was an idiot, which really made me mad.

"Are you kidding?" Stench sputtered incredulously. "It would be right out in the open where anyone could take it!"

"What a lousy idea," Tadpole seconded.

"I'm afraid I have to agree." Plasma Girl shrugged.

"Actually, it's a brilliant idea," I said, making no attempt to hide how angry I was. We all knew Hal wasn't as smart as the rest of us, but there was an unspoken rule that none of us would ever let him know we knew that.

Now I just had to figure out how to transform his

NAME: Halogen Boy. **POWER:** Able to illuminate himself to the intensity of the brightest light. **LIMITATIONS:** Requires apple juice to achieve maximum intensity. **CAREER:** On call for emergencies at the lighthouse on Hero's Cape, Halogen Boy is also a member of the Junior Leaguers. **CLASSIFICATION:** We predict a bright future, in at least one respect.

idea into a brilliant solution.

"How so?" Stench said. He knew he'd gone over the line.

"The best place to hide anything is in plain sight," I informed them. "If anyone comes into the club to try and find it, they'll assume it's hidden and go crazy looking through every obscure spot they can think of. They'll never expect it to be sitting right out in the open. So that's exactly where we'll put it. Just like Hal suggested."

The look I gave them made it clear that they better agree.

"Uh, right," Tadpole reluctantly concurred. "Great idea, Hal."

"It's brilliant," agreed Plasma Girl, who was clearly upset that she had let herself get carried away.

"Definitely," Stench joined in, happy at least that the card would stay in the headquarters.

Halogen Boy beamed brightly as the aquarium was lifted up and the card was set down right between the doorknob and the sardine can. Then the meeting quickly came to an end. We were all too upset about the fight. With only brief good-byes, we lowered the rope ladder and each of us headed for home.

CHAPTER EIGHTEEN

You're Never Too Old

I walked home feeling low. What should have been a moment of triumph—the completion of our AI Collector Card set—had been ruined by a fight. And I still wanted to know who had stolen the second card, and why.

When I got home the house was empty. Mom never got home from work before five, but I did expect Dad to be here. I looked in the family room and the living room, but I couldn't find any sign of him. And then I heard voices coming from the backyard. I went out the kitchen door and peeked through the garage door window. That was where I found my father—along with a few visitors.

"I know you're all wondering why I've gathered you here," my dad said to his three guests: the Big

Bouncer; the Levitator; and Stench's dad, Windbag. "The reason is I think it's high time we started our own team."

"Are you nuts?" said Windbag as he pulled a big fistful of potato chips out of a bag. "We're a bunch of middle-aged guys. What are we going to call ourselves: The Potbellied Posse?"

"Speak for yourself," said the Levitator, watching Windbag shove the chips into his mouth. "Thermo and I have both maintained our fighting trim—and I think it's a great idea. Remember how well we worked together when we were younger and members of the New Crusaders? We were unstoppable!"

"Exactly," my father agreed. "There's more talent sitting in this garage right now than in the entire League of Ultimate Goodness. If they don't want us, I say we start a rival group and show 'em who's the best. What do you think, BB?"

"Well," the Big Bouncer said, "I sure don't feel like I'm washed up. Windbag and I may look like two old fat guys, but we were this hefty when we were teenagers."

"Speak for yourself," huffed Windbag. "I wore a size fifty-two when I was in college, and now I'm down to a fifty-one."

"I don't know, though." The Big Bouncer sighed.

"Maybe these younger teams are right in thinking we're over the hill."

"Are you kidding?" my dad blurted out. "Remember all the stupid things we used to do when we were that age? We were idiots!"

"I remember, Hot Hands!" the Levitator said. They all started laughing, and my dad turned red. "Like the time you fell in the tank at the Seafood Hut and cooked their entire stock of lobsters!"

I tried to keep from laughing so they wouldn't discover I was there. I didn't want to miss any other good embarrassing stories about my dad.

"The point is"—my dad raised his voice over the chuckles—"our brains and experience more than make up for our lack of youth."

"But how will we make any money at it?" insisted the Big Bouncer. "You know that AI and the LUG's get all the rich endorsement deals."

"Yeah," the Levitator agreed. "You're lucky that Snowflake rakes in all that dough at Corpsicle. Windbag's junkyard may not make him rich, but he's also got what Chrysanthemum makes from her perfume business. But BB needs his job at the Mighty Mart, and I've only just gotten my delivery business off the ground. . . . Get it? Off the ground?"

Everybody groaned and rolled their eyes as the

Levitator cracked himself up.

"I'm not saying we quit our jobs—at least those of us who have jobs," my dad insisted. "We'd start up part-time and see how things work. Who knows, maybe we'll do well enough that we *can* quit our jobs— uh, I mean for those of us who haven't already quit their jobs—and take our lives in a bold new direction!"

"Okay, sure," Windbag said, casually reaching back and scratching his butt. "It'll get me out of the house whenever my wife expects me to take care of things."

"Count me in, Thermo," the Big Bouncer said. "What have I got to lose?"

"I'll do it, too," added the Levitator, "but what will we call ourselves?"

"I hadn't thought about it yet," my dad admitted, "but we need something punchy."

"How about the Fatalistic Four?" suggested Windbag.

"No, no, no," my father disagreed. "We may want to add additional members."

"We could call ourselves the League of Ultimate Geezers," joked the Levitator.

"I sort of like the Dream Team," recommended the Big Bouncer.

"No, that makes it sound like we spend most of our time sleeping in front of the TV," my dad said. "We need something daring and original, something that recalls our previous experience while taking us solidly into a bold new future."

He suddenly rose to his feet. "And I think I have it!"

I leaned closer to the door, eager to hear my dad's brainstorm.

"We'll call ourselves"—he paused for dramatic effect—"the New New Crusaders!"

CHAPTER NINETEEN

What Goes Up . . .

I tried not to think about the awful name my dad had given his new team. At school the next morning, my priority was to see that my team's fight was behind us. I ran into Plasma Girl and Tadpole just as I reached the main entrance. Before we could even say good morning, the school bus pulled up and Halogen Boy stepped out.

"Hey, guys." He greeted us as if nothing bad had happened yesterday. "Is the card still safe?"

"Stench isn't here yet," I replied, "but I'm sure it's fine."

"I hope he leaves it at headquarters." Plasma Girl shuddered slightly. "I don't want it causing us any more trouble here at school."

"You're right," Tadpole agreed. "Something as awesomely valuable as that will just tempt someone if we keep showing it off. After all, at best, there's only one other in existence."

"Hey guyth, gueth what I got my handth on?"

Turning around, we all got sprayed with seeds as Melonhead approached us. Normally it would have annoyed us, but this time we were too stunned by what he was holding—a Professor Brain-Drain card identical to our own.

"He stole our card!" Tadpole shouted.

Before anyone could stop him, he had pounced on Melonhead, and they both fell onto the pavement. Tadpole was on top and, I believe, trying to wrap his hands around Melonhead's neck. Of course since Melonhead's neck is actually the widest part of his head, Tadpole wasn't going to get anywhere with that. Nevertheless, Melonhead fought back the best way he knew how, and Tadpole found himself being pummeled with watermelon seeds to such an extent that he had no choice but to back off, shielding his face from the barrage of miniature projectiles.

"Great thethame! Thtop athaulting me," Melonhead sputtered. "Thith ithn't your card, for crimany thaketh!"

"What else could it be," Tadpole hollered as me and Hal restrained him.

"There *is* another card, Tadpole," Plasma Girl

165

reminded him. "Maybe Melonhead found it."

"Egthactly," Melonhead said as he got back on his feet. "Ekthept I didn't find it in a thtore. I bought it from thith weird-looking guy who offered it to me on the thtreet. I paid him twenty dollarth for it."

"Then *he* must have stolen it from us!" Tadpole raged as we continued to hold him down.

Just then Stench arrived. He didn't even have time to speak before Tadpole shouted at him.

"Someone stole our card that you were supposed to keep safe!"

"It is safe," Stench said, looking completely confused. "I saw it less than ten minutes ago. It's just where we left it."

"Thee!" Melonhead sprayed a slew of seeds directly into Tadpole's face before picking up his book bag and stomping off. In my opinion Tadpole deserved it. Before we could explain anything to Stench, the school bell rang and we all had to go inside.

Seeing Melonhead with the other card had been somewhat disturbing, but at least it was possible. What we discovered once we got inside the classroom was cataclysmically, impossibly disastrous.

"Look what I found," the Spore wheezed as he held up a Professor Brain-Drain card already covered in mildew. "I only had to pay ten dollars for it."

"You're kidding! I paid twenty-five dollars for mine," Cannonball complained, coming in right behind me. Sure enough, he had one, too.

"Mine cost me fifty dollars," wailed Lobster Boy. "Plus my bike."

Just then Transparent Girl came into the room. She had faded away to nothing but a pale outline, with the exception of her brand-new Professor Brain-Drain card.

"Look what I have," she said. "I tried to get it in exchange for my twenty-six AI cards, but the man who sold it to me wouldn't believe that I didn't have any money—partly because he could see the bills in my pocket. I ended up paying everything I had—sixty dollars. But it was worth it."

"Really?" I said, at least getting some small amusement out of this catastrophe. "Just look around."

Transparent Girl didn't need to be visible for me to imagine her mouth dropping open at the sight of a class full of Professor Brain-Drain cards. Puddle Boy was now displaying his as well.

"I bought three," he informed no one in particular. "The other two are safe in collector bags."

As usual, the room was in an uproar when Miss Marble arrived. It took all her skills to get everyone to sit down in their seats.

"If everyone doesn't calm down, I'll have Principal Doppelganger down here in two seconds flat," she threatened. "Now what's causing the commotion this morning?"

"We've all found Professor Brain-Drain cards," Cannonball announced proudly. "Now we're all rich!"

"Is that so?" Miss Marble said as she gave me a sideways glance. From the look on her face I could tell

she found this development as odd as I did.

"And just what did you pay for yours?" she asked Cannonball.

"Only twenty-five dollars," he said proudly.

The class once again erupted as everyone began shouting out how much he or she had paid. I gave a befuddled look to Stench and Plasma Girl, both of whom just shrugged. At that moment the Banshee shrieked that she had paid a hundred dollars for her card. As I wondered where she would have even gotten a hundred dollars, I felt a telltale rigidity running through my body. We had achieved a brand-new record in bad class behavior.

"Okay, students," Miss Marble said, rather calmly and patiently considering the situation. "Today you're going to learn why we make children go to school. It is precisely to prevent you from doing the incredibly stupid sort of thing that you all did this morning."

Miss Marble can sometimes be insulting, but today I think she had a point.

"As I said yesterday," she continued, "and as all of you clearly forgot—assuming your brains even absorbed it to begin with . . ."

"I absorbed it," volunteered the Human Sponge, whose porous lips allowed her to mumble somewhat despite being frozen.

Miss Marble continued uninterrupted. " . . . the value of something depends on how much supply there is compared with the demand for it."

At this moment we all began to unfreeze.

"Let me give you an example that you will all understand," she said gravely. "Yesterday there was lots of demand for a Professor Brain-Drain card and very little supply. That made it valuable. Let's see what the situation is like today."

I knew where this was headed, and it wasn't going to be pretty.

"How many of you have a Professor Brain-Drain card?"

Every hand in the class shot up.

"How many of you need a Professor Brain-Drain card?"

I turned around. Nobody put a hand up. Well, at least not at first. Then I heard some whispering and I turned back to the front to see Halogen Boy holding up his hand.

"I don't have one of my own yet."

"I'll sell you mine for eighty dollars," Transparent Girl offered him, with no sense of shame whatsoever. I had to at least give her credit for figuring out where things were heading.

"Don't even think about it," Plasma Girl hissed at her menacingly.

Miss Marble continued with her lesson. "So, Cannonball, what do you think your card is worth?"

"At least twenty-five dollars," he stated.

"And who would be willing to pay you that for it?"

"Halogen Boy?" he asked hopefully.

"I'll sell Hal mine for twenty dollars," Transparent Girl shouted out in undisguised desperation.

"Thikthteen dollarth, Hal," Melonhead spluttered. "Ith a thteal!"

"I'll sell him mine for ten dollars," huffed the Spore, trying to brush the mold off his card.

"You can have all three of my cards for five dollars," Puddle Boy said with anxiety as the puddle below his desk grew before our eyes. "And I'll even throw in the collector bags."

At this point panic had set in throughout the room.

"I'll sell you mine for a dollar—and a bike," said Lobster Boy not fully grasping his bargaining position.

"I'll sell him mine for a dime!" wailed the Banshee in complete despair. As I plugged my ears, I marveled at how something purchased for one hundred dollars had fallen to a dime in less than an hour.

Halogen Boy fished a dime out of his pocket and handed it to the Banshee, and she transferred her formerly valuable Professor Brain-Drain card to him.

"And that's what happens when supply is greater than demand," Miss Marble concluded with a bit more of a smile on her face than good teaching required.

Everyone in class sat in stunned silence, contemplating their now-worthless Professor Brain-Drain cards.

"But don't feel too bad, kids," Miss Marble consoled them. "Most of your parents never learned this lesson either. Just ask them about the stock market."

I didn't think she needed to be quite so smug, but I had to admit it was a lesson in economics that no one was going to forget soon. Meanwhile, I had a more pressing question on my mind. Where had all these cards come from?

CHAPTER TWENTY

Hot on the Trail

At lunchtime my team got together to discuss some-thing even more important than the sudden explosion of Professor Brain-Drain cards.

"I don't know about the rest of you," I began, "but last night I felt lousy after the fight we had."

"Me, too," admitted Plasma Girl. "And I'm not even sure what the fight was about."

"It was about who would hold on to the card," Tadpole snapped at her, as if that justified things.

"That's a dumb thing to fight over," said Stench.

"But the card is . . ." Tadpole's voice trailed off as he noticed us all scowling at him. He wisely decided not to push his point.

"It's not even worth anything," Plasma Girl pointed out. "At least not anymore."

"Is it still safe where we left it?" Halogen Boy asked. With his eyes hidden behind his dark goggles it was never easy to tell exactly what Hal's expression was, but I could tell he was concerned about the success of his idea for hiding (or not hiding) our Professor Brain-Drain card.

"It's safe, Hal. But in the end, the card doesn't really matter," I added. "What matters is our friendship. The Junior Leaguers are a team and we're dedicated to battling all wrongs . . . or at least the ones that occur before bedtime and don't interfere with our favorite TV shows. Just because adults squabble all the time, there's no reason for us to behave like that. Are we agreed?"

I stuck out my hand with my palm facing down, rolled my fingers into a fist, but left my thumb pointing out. Plasma Girl did the same, wrapping her fingers around my thumb. Halogen Boy and Stench quickly added to the circle and did likewise. Tadpole paused for only a moment and then wrapped his fist around Stench's thumb and inserted his own thumb into my fist. The circle was complete and we were once again a team.

"Agreed!" we all shouted in unison.

"And are the Junior Leaguers going to let this mystery go unsolved?" I asked.

"Never!" they responded as we unlinked our hands and prepared to do battle.

The problem, of course, was that none of us had a clue what had happened. Someone had obviously managed to create a whole slew of Professor Brain-Drain card duplicates, but how? It was while we were all racking our brains that we suddenly heard Cannonball shout from across the playground.

"Hey, there's the creep who sold me the phony card!"

We all turned to look and caught a glimpse of a tall figure in a long, black flowing cloak, wearing a wide-brimmed hat pulled down over his face. He was in the process of trying to sell a card to an unsuspecting kid from another class. As soon as he knew he'd been spotted, he whipped off the cloak and hat and vanished into thin air.

"Get him," hollered Lobster Boy. "He'll be riding a bike with clawed-up handlebars."

"Let'th thtring up the thuthpithiouth thtinker," agreed Melonhead.

All of a sudden a mob of angry eight- to twelve-year-olds ran toward the spot where the stranger had last been seen. Stench and Tadpole were about to join, when I hollered for them to stop. We had already lost sight of the stranger.

"Don't bother," I said in frustration. "He's already gone."

"Who do you think you saw, O Boy?" Plasma Girl asked.

"You guys will think I'm nuts, but I think it was the same guy I saw at Aunty Penny's Arcade. The one who stole the box of card packs."

"Then let's find that creep," Tadpole said with determination.

"We have to," I agreed, "but whoever it is, he's too clever to be caught by a screaming mob of grade-schoolers. Everyone else went that way"—I pointed—"so I say we go the opposite way. C'mon!"

The five of us took off in the general direction of downtown. It was only after we had left the school grounds that I realized we were in the midst of committing a major act of hooky. It was only noon, and leaving school before three o'clock was strictly forbidden. Nevertheless, I knew this was too important a lead for us to ignore. We had to find out who was selling these cards.

"Which way do you think he went?" Stench asked as we approached Colossal Way, the city's main east-west avenue. One direction led out to Telomere Park, the other straight into downtown Superopolis.

"This way," Halogen Boy said. "I think I see some-thing."

Turning toward downtown, the rest of us immediately caught sight of what appeared to be a riderless bicycle five or six blocks ahead. "It's Lobster Boy's bike!" shouted Tadpole. We began to run faster, but there was no way we could keep up with a bicycle. We kept after it for almost ten blocks until we were once again traveling along the south side of Lava Park. It was there that we finally lost sight of it altogether. Exhausted, we all collapsed beneath a statue of an enormous potato chip.

I realized we were back at the Inkblot's Newsstand. I blinked. And then I blinked again. For there, right in front of my eyes, was the answer.

"That's it!" I said.

"What's it?" Plasma Girl asked between breaths.

"The answer to the mystery is right in front of us," I said.

"The Inkblot is the answer to the mystery?" Stench replied, baffled.

I thought the newspapers hung out on the Inkblot's stand said it all: MULTIPLIER ESCAPES! screamed *The Hero Herald*; MISSTEPS AT MAXIMUM EMANCIPATE MULTIPLIER blared *The Superopolis Times*. Then, of course, there was also *The Weekly Daily*, once again living up to its motto of "Last Week's News Today" with the headline: MULTIPLIER MAKES MESS OF MIGHTY MART. Sadly, my teammates just stared at the newspapers blankly.

"Don't you see it?" I said. "The Multiplier could have made all those duplicate cards. And he escaped from prison just yesterday."

"He looks like a complete loser," Tadpole commented as he picked up a copy of *The Hero Herald* to examine more closely. That was all it took for the Inkblot to notice us. He turned his attention away from a squirrel he apparently had been talking to and instead focused on us. The squirrel wasted no time in escaping.

"So like I was saying, Captain Radio was the greatest hero of all time," he started to say, seemingly unaware that there had been almost a two-day gap since our last conversation. "But even he couldn't withstand the power of the Red Menace. Now there was an evil genius! His voice alone could make people do things against their will."

"What about the Tycoon?" Stench asked me. "He could have printed up more cards just to irritate us."

"No, that would have cost him money," Plasma Girl pointed out.

The Inkblot kept right on talking, oblivious to whether anyone was paying attention. "As the Red Menace realized the extent of his power he got bolder. He corrupted Captain Radio and used the captain's powers to broadcast his evil instructions to everyone in Superopolis. He told everyone that they didn't have to work anymore. Well, people liked that message for a while—at least until the grocery stores ran out of potato chips and pizza places started taking two months to deliver pizzas and no one picked up the trash anymore. The price of a banana reached four hundred and seventy-one dollars at one point. But it was all part of his master plan."

In a way, what I heard of the Inkblot's story was fascinating, and normally I would have even enjoyed listening. But I had a feeling we were closing in on a huge break in this case and I needed to focus.

"Luckily, there were still some heroes who were smart enough to get their news from the papers instead of the radio. Five of them—just like you young whippersnappers—gathered together and formed the League of Goodness."

My ears perked up at this, but I was busy arguing with Stench. "It's too much of a coincidence," I insisted. "The Multiplier escapes and all of a sudden we have multiple copies of Professor Brain-Drain cards? In this instance, one plus one clearly equals the Multiplier."

"That's addition, not multiplication," Halogen Boy pointed out.

"I think you're right," Stench agreed, ignoring Hal. "Only the Multiplier could have made all these duplicates. But how do we find him?"

I pulled out my copy of the *Li'l Hero's Handbook*.

"Even without my help," the Inkblot admitted to no one in particular, "they managed to put an end to the Red Menace's reign of terror and lock him away in a soundproof room. After that, they became the most famous heroes in Superopolis, while Captain Radio was disgraced and forced into retirement."

I think the Inkblot muttered something like "served him right," but I was busy flipping through the appendices in the back of my handbook. Ah, here was what I was looking for! Secret hideouts!

"According to the *Li'l Hero's Handbook*, the Multiplier's secret hideout is at Seventeen Skullduggery Lane," I informed everyone.

"What a terrible neighborhood," Tadpole commented. "He must not be a very competent villain if that's the best he can afford to rent."

"It makes perfect sense," I agreed. "He never has been very successful—at least until now. What I can't figure out is how he managed to pull his stunt at the Mighty Mart, escape from prison, and now create all these duplicate Professor Brain-Drain cards. What's changed him?"

"There's only one way to find out," Plasma Girl said, speaking for all of us. "It's time to pay a visit to Seventeen Skullduggery Lane."

CHAPTER TWENTY-ONE
A Minuscule Threat

I turned to apologize to the Inkblot for having to run, but he was now shouting at a picture of Mayor Whitewash on the cover of *Superopolis Style* magazine, and clearly wouldn't notice us leaving.

"Come on, gang!" I hollered. "We're back in hot pursuit!"

We headed toward one of the seediest parts of downtown Superopolis and soon found Skullduggery Lane. Most of the buildings on the street seemed to be warehouses. There were all sorts of shady characters loading and unloading what I imagined to be ill-gotten gains and illegal thingamajigs.

When we got to number 17, it looked like all the other buildings, except there was no activity going on. What we did find, however, was a bike leaning against the side of the building. And not just any bike. We could tell by the clawed-up handlebars that this was none other than Lobster Boy's bike. Whoever sold him the phony card must be inside. We peeked through a window, but we weren't able to see anything. I tried the heavy metal door, but it wouldn't budge.

"Stench"—I gestured to the door—"would you mind doing the honors?"

"My pleasure," he said as he strode up to the door, grabbed hold of the handle, and yanked the door off its hinges with one effortless tug.

Unfortunately, Stench's exertion brought with it a small burst of gas. We all held our breaths and quickly ran into the dark warehouse.

"Hal, can you give us some light?" I asked.

In response, he took a quick swig from his sippy cup. Soon he began to glow, the dimness vanished, and the items piled all around us became perfectly clear. Our mouths dropped open in amazement. The warehouse was filled with stacks and stacks of traffic cones and crates full of traffic cones everywhere we looked. Thousands of them! No, *hundreds* of thousands of them! What could possibly be the point?

"What's with all the traffic cones?" Stench said.

"I have no idea," I said, since I had no idea.

"Maybe the Multiplier has been making them,"

suggested Plasma Girl, her mouth hanging open in awe.

"But it would have taken him ages to create all these. Most of these cones look like they've been here for years. Just look at all the dust on them."

"What would anyone want with a gazillion traffic cones anyway?" Tadpole asked.

"I don't know," I said as I led the way farther into the warehouse, "but we're going to find out."

The team followed me deeper and deeper into the warehouse, passing between towers of cones, sometimes piled fifty feet high. Soon we saw a light ahead that became brighter and brighter as we got closer. I whispered to Hal to douse his own light and I cautiously poked my head over the nearest bunch of traffic cones. What I saw confirmed everything I had suspected.

There, in a clear space within the warehouse, was the Multiplier. And hanging from the ceiling by a thin wire was a clamp. Clutched by the clamp, I could tell even from where we were hiding, was a Professor Brain-Drain card. Instinctively, I knew it was the second genuine card in existence—the one stolen from Aunty Penny's Arcade. The Multiplier was pinching the card between his thumb and index finger. As I watched him concentrate, a duplicate of the card appeared out of thin air in his other hand. He set it down on a stack of duplicate cards about two inches high and then once again began lightly pinching the original. I barely even breathed. It must have taken nearly five minutes, but sure enough, another card appeared in his empty hand. The duplicating speed that I had witnessed in the Mighty Mart the other day had clearly been abnormal.

All of a sudden, I swore I heard a voice mumble something. Then the Multiplier responded. It sounded like he was talking to someone, but I couldn't see anyone else. He possibly could have been talking to himself, but the Multiplier wasn't supposed to be crazy—just incompetent. I motioned for the team to stay where they were while I tried to move closer. I had to hear what was being said.

I moved around to within a few feet of where the Multiplier was standing. I could see only part of him, since my view was partly blocked by the crates, but I could hear him perfectly. And he definitely wasn't alone.

"I'm creating them as fast as I can," he was complaining in a whiny voice. "Since I escaped from prison I haven't even had a chance to sleep!"

"You ssseem to forget that it was I who ssset you free," hissed the eeriest voice I had ever heard.

"I know. And I appreciate it," the Multiplier said nervously, obviously afraid of whoever he was talking to. "But I've been making these cards all night. Can I help it that my power is slow?"

"You were given a devissse to ssspeed up the prosssesss," the stranger reminded him. "However, your sssilly essscapade at the grosssery ssstore dessstroyed it. It wasss one of a kind and will take time to replassse. It'sss a shame you weren't sssmart enough to duplicate it firssst."

I could glimpse enough of the foolish expression on the Multiplier's face to see that something so simple had never occurred to him. And then my mind flashed back to the thing I had seen him drop as he sailed across the checkout area of the Mighty Mart. One mystery solved.

"In the meantime, I need more cardsss," the voice continued. "You've only sssupplied usss with hundredsss, while we need millionsss. Bring what you have to headquartersss in two hoursss. Perhapsss a new devissse will be ready for you then. Don't messs up again."

I could tell that the mysterious figure had departed by the expression of relief that spread across the Multiplier's face. What I had overheard the stranger say to the Multiplier, however, was astounding.

Millions of cards?! What had we stumbled upon? There weren't enough kids in all Superopolis to possibly justify making millions of Professor Brain-Drain cards. And who was this mysterious stranger? It had to be the same person who had stolen the card from right beneath our noses at Aunty Penny's Arcade and sold duplicate cards to all our unsuspecting classmates. But the money he had made off them couldn't have added up to more than a thousand dollars (and Lobster Boy's bike). There had to be something more at stake. Unfortunately, I wasn't going to find out what just yet, because at exactly that moment a loud noise pierced the silence of the warehouse. It was a noise that I knew could have come from only one person.

"Stench!" I muttered softly to myself in irritation.

I risked peeking around the cones, only to see the Multiplier darting off in the direction from which the unpleasant noise had come. I followed right behind, screeching to a halt along with him as he spotted my four teammates huddled in front of a crate. I could tell from their teary eyes that they had all gotten a power-ful whiff of Stench's mistake. It had left them all a bit disoriented. When they caught sight of the Multiplier, they all panicked.

Tadpole turned and ran smack into a tall stack of crates filled with traffic cones. High above, the top crate shuddered and moved. Then Halogen Boy smashed into the same stack and the top crate was jarred from its perch. All four of the confused heroes looked up at the crate as it tumbled toward them, its open side facing down. Right in front of the Multiplier, the crate landed like a cage on top of the trespassers.

"I don't know who you kids are, but you'll regret having tangled with the Multiplier," he said, with a halfhearted evil laugh. "This will calm you down until I can figure out what to do about you."

Once again I was helpless—a kid with no power who could do nothing but watch as the Multiplier dug a capsule out of his pocket and forced it through a hole in the crate. A minute later I saw whiffs of a cloudy gas leaking from cracks all over the box and I knew my friends had been knocked unconscious.

Having no power left me with two options. I could wallow in my helplessness and run away. Or I could stop feeling sorry for myself and do what a hero should do. The choice was obvious; there was no way I was going to abandon my friends. I launched myself right at the Multiplier.

"AIIIEEE!!" he shrieked, as I tackled him.

For a moment, I actually believed that, even with no power, I might be able to take someone as incompetent as the Multiplier. But he quickly turned on me, which wasn't difficult considering he was twice my size. I struggled to get away, but he grabbed hold of my belt with one hand and hauled me back. He wrapped his arm around my torso, trapped my arms, and held me motionless. Within a few minutes, a duplicate of my belt appeared in his other hand and he soon had it strapped around my chest and arms.

My feelings of powerlessness once again overwhelmed me. It was bad enough that we had all been captured, but it was positively humiliating that we had been caught by someone the *Li'l Hero's Handbook* classified as "a minuscule threat."

CHAPTER TWENTY-TWO

At the Mercy of The Multiplier

I watched in frustration as the Multiplier dragged each of my unconscious teammates out from under the crate and tied them up tightly. He then disappeared into the warehouse while I helplessly looked on. All of a sudden Stench opened one eye and winked at me. I was relieved to see that he at least had already recovered.

"I've sort of developed a natural immunity to powerful gasses," he whispered. "Should I break these ropes and bring this creep down?"

"Keep playing like you're knocked out," I whispered back. "I want to get as much information out of him as possible. Tell the others, too, when they wake up. And don't let them do anything yet to reveal their powers."

"You got it, O Boy," Stench whispered back.

The Multiplier returned shortly, pushing an enormous machine on wheels.

"What's that?" I asked him, genuinely curious.

"It's a device that was left behind here by an old supervillain named the Red Menace," the Multiplier explained. "He rented this space before me. He left behind cases and cases of stuff he'd collected. I had it all hauled away to the dump except for this thing."

I suddenly remembered that the Red Menace was the villain that the Inkblot had just been rambling on about. Now I wished I'd paid a little more attention.

"What does it do?" I asked. The machine was big and nasty looking. Not only was there a long conveyor belt that led through a series of presses and stompers and mashers and crushers, but there were huge copper kettles linked by coiled hoses situated right in the middle of the monstrosity.

"According to the instruction booklet left with it, it was supposed to be used to make something the Red Menace called 'the fuel of the revolution,'" the Multiplier announced importantly. He clearly had no better idea than I did what the thing was for. "It says to dump potatoes onto the conveyor belt and then turn the machine on. It does all the rest."

"Why would anyone use potatoes for anything

other than making potato chips?" I asked.

"I don't know," the Multiplier snapped back. "My plan is to strap you kids to the belt and turn the thing on."

"And why would you do that?" I asked as calmly as possible.

"Because that's what a villain is supposed to do," he shrieked. "It says so in my handbook!"

To my complete and utter surprise, the Multiplier held up a handbook almost identical to my *Li'l Hero's Handbook*. As he brought the book closer to me, I saw that someone had had the audacity to publish something called the *Li'l Villain's Handbook*.

"Who would publish something like that!" I said, outraged.

The Multiplier attempted an evil leer as he stepped up to me and showed me the name on the back of the book: *The Gibraltar Press, a division of Indestructo Industries*. I should have known.

"This book is great!" the Multiplier enthused. "I just picked it up last week and it's given me all sorts of good advice."

"Excuse me?" I said in disgust. "Didn't that advice get you

sent to jail? I would hardly call that a success."

"But look at all this great press I'm getting for the first time in my life," he insisted, holding up a batch of newspapers with his name on the front pages.

"An obituary is great press, too," I added. "And who was that guy that you're making the fakes for?" I demanded despite being in no position to demand anything.

"How much did you overhear?" the Multiplier asked nervously. "You're better off not knowing anything about it."

"It's too late for that," I answered. "I know where that card you're duplicating came from, because my friends and I have the only other genuine one in existence. Your copies have made this our business."

"Actually, the problem is that I can't make copies of the card fast enough," he informed me.

"What about your little show at the Mighty Mart?" I accused. "I was there when you created all those toilet paper rolls at lightning speed. In fact it was my dad who stopped you."

"You're the Amazing Indestructo's kid!" the Multiplier shrieked with a look of complete terror on his face.

"No!" I said in disgust. Even the Multiplier had forgotten who really captured him. "Never mind. The point is that you suddenly had an awful lot of power then that you don't have now."

"Well there's no reason not to tell you," he admitted, "since you'll all be turned into the 'fuel of the revolution' soon.

"You may find this hard to believe," he said, "but people have often underestimated me."

"Do tell?" I said, pretending shock.

"It's true." He nodded in confirmation. "Yet I've always considered myself a major villain."

"People's perceptions of themselves are often at odds with reality," I pointed out helpfully.

"Exactly," the Multiplier agreed, completely missing my insult. "So I decided it was time for me to make the world tremble before my power. The problem, however, was that my master plan wasn't yet ready."

The Multiplier vaguely indicated the enormous stacks piled throughout the warehouse.

"The traffic cones?" I asked.

"Exactly," he replied as if that should explain everything. "I still need even more. Luckily, I was offered a device that could speed up my powers dramatically. All I had to do in exchange for it was to create millions of copies of that card. The problem was that the person who gave me the device didn't yet have the card he wanted copied. So I had a chance to try the device out first on my own."

"And that's when you went to the Mighty Mart," I concluded.

"I had gone there to buy up packs of cards—and some toilet paper. I was all out. I had just gotten to the paper goods," he started to fume, "when some little kid suddenly pointed at me and began laughing."

"So you had to show off your new power."

He nodded. "No one will be laughing once I execute my master plan, though." He raised his hands in the air triumphantly, indicating the traffic cones all around him.

"What exactly *is* your plan?" I asked, genuinely fascinated.

"It's pure genius!" The Multiplier cackled. "I've been planning this for over ten years. Each duplicate cone takes me five minutes to create. I can make twelve of them each hour, and I spend twelve hours a day making them. I've done it every day for ten years. The only days I've taken off are Christmas and Groundhog Day, and I now have over half a million cones. I figure I only need a couple hundred thousand more."

He looked at me as if the rest of his plan should be obvious.

"And . . . ?" I said.

"I should have known it was too brilliant to be apparent to a mere child." He sighed. "The cones are to redirect traffic."

I still had no idea what he was talking about.

"And . . . ?"

"And with enough of them, I can redirect all traffic away from Superopolis. The city will be empty and I can rob every place in town and steal everything I want." His voice became higher and more excited as he spoke. He followed up with that same evil laugh that he still needed to work on.

My mouth dropped open at the stupidity of his plan. In fact it was so moronic it almost took idiocy to the level of an art form. As I glanced around at all the traffic cones, I couldn't help but think they were

suddenly looking like an enormous collection of dunce caps.

"What if superheroes just ignore the cones and go right past them into the city?" I asked.

The Multiplier paused for a moment, looking like he was pondering that possibility for the very first time—which I'm sure he was. His face became purple with rage. "You're just like the rest," he shrieked louder than ever. "You refuse to see the brilliance of my plan! Well, soon it won't matter."

With that he picked up the still-unconscious Halogen Boy and hauled him over to the conveyor belt where he strapped him on top of it. As he did the same with Plasma Girl and Tadpole, Stench once again whispered to me.

"Is it time for me to act?"

"Not yet." I shook my head. "I'm still not completely certain who's behind this, although I have a pretty good idea."

Stench once again closed his eyes as the Multiplier struggled to lift him onto the conveyor belt. I heard an audible crack, and the Multiplier let out a groan as he strapped Stench down. Finally, he shuffled over to me, obviously in some pain.

"I regret that you won't be able to see the glorious success of my master plan," he said. The fact that he made me walk over to the machine myself and hop up on the conveyor belt told me that he wouldn't be doing any more heavy lifting anytime soon. "But as brilliant as the plan is," he continued as he strapped me down,

"I have to admit, it wasn't *my* idea alone."

How could such a dumb plan have had two minds working on it—unless, of course, the other individual had his own plan in mind.

"In fact," he continued, "the original idea belonged to the same person I'm creating all these cards for. He suggested it to me the first time I met him, over ten years ago. Of course, I perfected the plan," he added.

At this point I had had enough.

"Did you ever stop to think," I asked the Multiplier, "that if you had spent the last ten years making duplicates of a single diamond, or a single gold bar, that you would now be the richest person in all Superopolis?"

The look of triumph on the Multiplier's face froze in place for a moment and then his expression went blank. How could *anyone* be so stupid? And then it hit me. Nobody could be born that big of an idiot. Someone had turned the Multiplier into a moron. Once I realized that, I knew exactly who he had gotten the idea from and who was behind this whole collector card crisis.

That's when the Multiplier, fuming with rage, turned on the machine.

CHAPTER TWENTY-THREE

Heroes to the End?

As the conveyor belt began to move, the Multiplier just stood there snickering at us.

"Umm, shouldn't you be going now?" I asked from where I lay strapped to the belt.

"Why?" he asked, a look of confusion on his face.

"Everyone knows that an evil genius never waits around to make sure his traps work," I informed him.

He looked at me suspiciously for a moment, but then the fact that I had actually referred to him as a genius sank in.

"I was just getting ready to go," he said, picking up the small stack of cards he had duplicated and retrieving the original card from the clamp. "Besides, it's time for me to deliver these cards and get my increased powers back. Today the cards, tomorrow

201

the cones!" He stabbed his finger into the air and let out a maniacal laugh. "And the day after that—all Superopolis!"

As he turned to leave, he tripped over one of the traffic cones and fell flat on his face. When he got back up he was muttering, which he kept doing as he wandered away into the dark. There was no sound of a slamming door, but then again, Stench had ripped it off its hinges. Which reminded me . . .

"Stench, it's all clear."

It took Stench two seconds to burst the straps that were wrapped around him.

As he hopped off the conveyor belt I thought he would begin rescuing the others, but then it became

clear there was no need. The rest of my team members had been faking unconsciousness as well. Plasma Girl simply liquefied herself and slithered off the belt. At the same time, Tadpole's tongue snaked over to the front of the machine and with no effort at all snapped the machine's switch into the off position.

"That guy'th an idiot," said Tadpole before his tongue was fully back in his mouth.

"You're right," I agreed. "Which is the final clue I needed to figure out who's really behind this."

"Is it that strange person the Multiplier was talking to?" asked Halogen Boy.

"That's what I thought at first," I said, "but then I realized that he's only working for someone as well."

"But if it's not him," insisted Plasma Girl, "then who is it?"

"Who is smart enough to hire others to do his dirty work?" I asked. "Who has the intelligence to create a device that can amplify the Multiplier's power? Who has the ability to sap the intelligence of someone to the extent that he would spend ten years of his life plotting a crime involving traffic cones? Even the Multiplier couldn't have been that naturally stupid. And finally . . ."

They all leaned in toward me.

"Who has every reason to be mad that only three

cards were made with his picture on them?"

"Professor Brain-Drain!" they all said in unison.

"Precisely," I said. "And now it's time we confronted him directly."

"Are you kidding?" said Stench.

"We can't take on Professor Brain-Drain," agreed Tadpole.

"O Boy, even the Amazing Indestructo barely triumphs over the Professor," Plasma Girl fretted. "What could *we* be expected to accomplish? We couldn't even take on the Multiplier!"

"That's just because we played dead," Hal responded, sticking up for us all. "We could have taken him in a second, if O Boy hadn't thought it was more important to get information out of him."

"That's true," Plasma Girl agreed. "But Professor Brain-Drain is different. How do we stop him from draining our intelligence? You saw what happened to the Multiplier."

Plasma Girl didn't have to direct our attention to the hundreds of thousands of traffic cones stacked throughout the warehouse. We all got her scary point.

"I may not have a power like you guys," I said, "but I know that a hero doesn't run away from danger. Professor Brain-Drain is up to something and we're the only ones who know about it. Would the Amazing

Indestructo give up? Of course not. So are we going to fight or not?"

My four teammates looked guiltily at each other. Sure, they were afraid of going after the most dangerous supervillain of all (heck, so was I!), but they were superheroes first and foremost. As they looked to each other for silent encouragement, I knew they would come to the right . . .

"No way," said Tadpole. "You saw what the Multiplier tried to do to us. What do you think Brain-Drain would do?"

"Fine," I said, letting them all see how disappointed with them I was. "I'll go after him myself."

I pulled out my copy of the *Li'l Hero's Handbook* and looked up Professor Brain-Drain in the appendix. It said that his secret headquarters were located on the top floor of the Vertigo Building. I slammed the book shut, slipped it into my back pocket, and turned to leave the warehouse.

I only made it a few feet before I heard a familiar voice behind me.

"I'll go with you, O Boy."

It was Halogen Boy. That was all it took. By the time I had made my way to the door, the other three Junior Leaguers had caught up with us.

"We won't desert you, either," Plasma Girl said.

"You're right. We're either heroes or we're not."

Tadpole and Stench nodded in agreement. I was incredibly proud of my teammates.

Unfortunately, things were about to get more complicated.

"Do you guys see what I see?" I asked them as we stood on the street outside the Multiplier's warehouse.

"What is it?" Tadpole asked.

"Take a look." I nodded my head toward Lobster Boy's bike, which was still leaning against the building.

"What about it?" said Stench. "It was there when we came in."

"Exactly," I said. "It was ridden down here by the mysterious person who stole the second card and sold the duplicates to our classmates—the one we overheard threatening the Multiplier. Obviously he's still here."

A shiver ran down our spines and we all looked around. Of course, there was no one to be seen. Whoever this stranger was, he had a remarkable ability to remain inconspicuous. Suddenly, I began to get a strong sense of who it was. I whispered in Stench's ear.

"Go and round up some help. I think we're going to need it," I said. "The rest of us will go to the Vertigo Building. If we're not waiting outside for you, come in with everything you've got."

"You got it, O Boy," he responded and headed off.

To be perfectly honest, I wasn't sure how much of a threat Professor Brain-Drain would actually be. Apart from what we saw on the Amazing Indestructo's TV show, the Professor seemed to keep a pretty low profile these days. Nevertheless, I thought it made sense to have backup in case this situation was more dangerous than I suspected. And I knew I could count on Stench.

"Let's go, team," I said to the rest of them, and we headed back toward downtown. I didn't turn around to check on Lobster Boy's bike as we left. If I had, it wouldn't have been nearly so shocking twenty minutes later when we arrived at the entrance to the Vertigo Building and found the bike parked outside.

THE VERTIGO BUILDING

Located in the heart of the Superopolis financial district, the Vertigo Building is perfectly situated to provide office space for hundreds of criminals and accountants. Owned by the nefarious Professor Brain-Drain, it is abundantly clear how he earned at least one of his many nicknames, the Landlord of Crime. Seventy-five stories high, it is the tallest building in Superopolis.

CHAPTER TWENTY-FOUR

Rising to the Challenge

"How did that get here?" Plasma Girl asked in alarm.

Sure enough, Lobster Boy's bike was now leaning against a lamppost in front of the Vertigo Building. Only this time it had a huge padlock on it—which in this case made perfect sense. You see, the Vertigo Building is home to hundreds and hundreds of supervillains. At seventy-five stories, it's the tallest building in Superopolis, and for some reason it became the spot of choice for villains looking for office space. Personally, if I were a supervillain, I would want something more . . . well . . . villain-ish than space in a skyscraper. But it's probably a good thing I don't think the same way as a criminal.

We all stared up at the enormous building. None of us had ever been this close to it before. What we saw

209

at the top, however, confirmed that we were in the right place, for tethered to the spire of the building was the Brain-Drain Blimp.

There was an incredible amount of activity going on around the building. All over the place villains were either coming back from crimes or heading out to commit them. Of the ones returning, some were carrying items they had stolen. Others appeared empty-handed. I recognized one of them; a guy dressed in ratty-looking clothes named Mr. Rotten, whose power was to spoil anything he touched. He was running toward the entrance carrying what looked like a bag of cash, but just before he reached it, a hero called the Jackhammer came pummeling out of the sky feetfirst, knocking Mr. Rotten to the ground. The bag of cash fell open, and we saw little crumbled pieces of bills blowing away. They had already rotted to almost nothing, which I'm sure had to be pretty depressing for a villain.

As the Jackhammer wrapped up Mr. Rotten in a garbage bag to avoid touching him, the rest of the villains around the Vertigo Building scattered like cockroaches. We figured this was our chance to make our way inside.

In the lobby we found a directory that must have had two hundred names on it. First we looked under *P* for Professor Brain-Drain, but there was no listing. Next we tried *B*, but still no luck.

"Jeesh," complained Tadpole, "what's the point of keeping a low profile when you've got a blimp with your name on it tied up to the building?"

"Good point," I agreed. "But it doesn't matter. We know he must be on the top floor. How else could he get into the blimp?"

We hadn't noticed, but Hal had wandered off toward a guard who was posted over in a corner of the lobby.

"Hal, stop!" Plasma Girl whispered as loudly as she could. The last thing we wanted to do was draw any attention to ourselves. But Hal didn't hear her. He walked right up to the guard.

"Where can we find Professor Brain-Drain?" he asked innocently.

"Seventy-fifth floor, kid," the guard said without even blinking. "Take any elevator. He's always happy to have guests."

As the guard said that, he started laughing in a way that made me very nervous.

Just then we heard a buzzer, and the door to one of the elevators slid open right in front of us. Sitting on a high stool by the controls was a guy with three arms. I noticed it right away, as one tends to do when encountering someone with an extra limb.

"Where to, kiddies?" he asked. Apparently he was the elevator operator.

"Seventy-fifth floor," I said as I ushered my reluctant group inside.

"Professor Brain-Drain, huh?" he grunted. "That's a *great* idea."

I didn't like the sound of that. But he was already pulling the door shut with one hand, punching the button for the seventy-fifth floor with the other, and pulling a lever to start the elevator rising with the third. There was a clank and a harsh metallic groan, and the cage slowly began to rise. It was not going to be a fast trip.

The elevator operator's third hand stayed on the lever, but his other two hands were now free. One of them fished a cigarette out of his shirt pocket, and the other retrieved a match. He puffed a big cloud of smoke into the enclosed space of the elevator.

"Hey, that's illegal," Plasma Girl complained.

"Oh, no!" he said, acting nervous. "I guess that makes me a . . . a criminal!"

Then he burst out laughing.

I guess there's not a whole lot you can do about someone breaking the law in a building filled with criminals. Nevertheless, the guy was really annoying us.

"Besides, if you're so worried about

your health," he continued, "you shouldn't be heading up to see Professor Brain-Drain."

Then he started laughing all over again. I had to admit I was getting more and more nervous about what we were getting ourselves into. But it was too late now. We had finally reached the seventy-fifth floor and the door was opening. The operator was still laughing as we stepped off the elevator, but that stopped as Tadpole's tongue darted out, wrapped itself around the leg of his stool, and yanked it out from underneath him. As he tumbled onto the floor with all three of his arms flailing in the air, Tadpole retracted his tongue, and the door closed once again. The operator's cursing faded quickly as the elevator descended.

The four of us found ourselves in an outer lobby. In front of us was a blank double door. I reached to grab one of the handles, but before I even touched it the doors swung open to reveal a person standing just inside.

"Welcome, my junior do-gooders. I've been expecting you."

Even if he hadn't looked exactly like the picture on his card, there would have been no mistaking Professor Brain-Drain this time.

CHAPTER TWENTY-FIVE

Brain-Drain's Lair

I knew that we were facing the genuine Professor Brain-Drain because he looked quite a bit older than he ever did in episodes of the *The Amazing Adventures of the Amazing Indestructo (and the League of Ultimate Goodness)* TV show. Plus the chill in my bones told me that this was the guy. The costume, of course, was just like it was on TV and in the comic books. He had on a brilliant white lab coat that came down to just below his knees. Underneath the open coat he was dressed completely in black. And, of course, on top of his bald head, he had on his trademark steel colander. I couldn't help but wonder for a moment if he ever took it off and used it to drain pasta.

"Welcome to my secret headquarters," he said, smiling rather pleasantly for a criminal mastermind. "It's always nice to have visitors—especially children. Please, come and sit down while I call for some refreshments."

It was difficult to see his expression through the enormously thick glasses he wore, but so far, he wasn't acting anything like an evil genius. Either he wasn't remotely as dangerous as AI made him out to be, or he was plotting something.

As we were ushered into the heart of his lair, our eyes nearly popped out. This wasn't just a single floor of an office building. The entire top of the skyscraper, all the way up into its spire, was completely hollow, reaching up as high as a hundred feet. At the very top were a series of catwalks that connected to a docking area for the enormous Brain-Drain blimp. A figure was moving about on the walkways, too far away to identify. My attention returned to the immediate surroundings. The entire space was jammed full of the most amazing array of machines and devices I had ever seen.

"You're looking at a lifetime of work," Professor Brain-Drain announced proudly as we all stared up at an enormous model of the solar system. It was actually revolving around the center of the space, apparently unconnected to anything. "Come, have a look."

He led us past what looked like a large steam pipe organ, except in place of the pipes there were a series of fireworks rockets. The Professor saw that I was looking at it and stopped to talk about it.

"I call that my Combustible Calliope," he said with a chuckle—not a chortle or a cackle, like on TV, but a chuckle. "So far I've been reluctant to play it since I fear the first time could be the last."

"Why's that?" asked Tadpole. "It looks pretty cool to me."

"The problem is all the explosives," the Professor said. "I'm convinced that they'll add a marvelous quality to the music, but who wants to be the one to try it out?"

I could tell from the look on Tadpole's face that he would *love* to try it out.

"What's that?" Halogen Boy asked, pointing to a contraption that looked like a bicycle equipped with wings.

"Oh, that's the Icarus III," answered the Professor with a wry smile. "You don't want to know what happened to the Icarus I and the Icarus II."

By this time we had reached the middle of the expansive space and we all caught sight of an enormous machine that dominated the center of the room.

"What does *that* thing do?" Halogen Boy asked,

wide-eyed. From the floor all the way up into the spire of the building stood what looked like a gigantic barber pole, at least ten feet wide. As the red-, white-, and blue-striped pole slowly turned, electrical bolts and currents flashed and sparked all around the top, making it look like the pole was spiraling up through the ceiling. On the floor, a series of chairs surrounded the pole, each with a metallic dome placed above it. Each dome had something like a gauge or a clock face set into it. More than anything, they looked like hair dryers from a beauty parlor.

"That's one of my hare-brained schemes." The Professor laughed. "No need to concern yourself with it just yet."

I hated to say it, but Professor Brain-Drain really seemed like a fairly nice guy. He led us into a sitting room in the corner, which had incredible views of the ocean to the east and downtown Superopolis to the north. There were also about half a dozen statues placed around the sitting room. They all looked like variations of Professor Brain-Drain himself.

"What are these statues?" I asked.

"Oh, just one of my hobbies," the Professor responded. "I've been through my painting stage and my pottery stage. Now I'm trying sculpture. I'm practicing first with self-portraits."

"They look so lifelike," Tadpole said, poking one of them in the stomach.

"Why thank you," the Professor said, seeming genuinely pleased as he ushered us to sit down and then took his own seat.

"First of all, what can I get you?" he asked. "I believe I have some lemonade and some homemade cookies. Does that sound suitable?"

We all nodded, confused by his hospitality.

"Excellent." He smiled. "The refreshments should be here soon. While we wait, let's discuss these pesky cards that seem to be causing you so much trouble."

"So you do know about them!" I said in a more accusing tone than I intended.

"Of course I do." The Professor smiled pleasantly. "The same way I knew you would be showing up here to discuss them with me. Here, please help yourselves to the cookies."

I noticed that a tray of cookies and a pitcher of lemonade had just appeared on the table as if out of nowhere.

"You see," Professor Brain-Drain continued, "I've had you observed since the moment you showed up at Indestructo Industries two days ago."

"By who?" I tried to ask casually. I had suspected as much myself, but I was surprised that he would

NAME: Sneak, The. **POWER:** Like a chameleon, the Sneak can blend into any background. **LIMITATIONS:** Being difficult to see is not always an asset. As an infant his parents lost him numerous times. This may have contributed to his antisocial criminal tendencies. **CAREER:** Briefly attempted a legitimate career as a traffic cop with disastrous results. Turned to crime thereafter. **CLASSIFICATION:** As an information gatherer, the Sneak is a master.

come right out and admit it.

"By me, little onesss," a familiar voice suddenly hissed from right next to me.

I spun around and looked right at where the voice had come from. There was nobody there! And then the wall moved. Well, actually the wall didn't move. A figure moved who was the same color and texture as the wall. He stepped away from it and stood in front of one of the windows. Within seconds, the figure began to change to a pale blue identical to the color of the sky outside the window.

"I'd like to introduce you kids to the Sneak," Professor Brain-Drain explained as he poured each of us a glass of lemonade. "He already feels like he knows you after spending most of Monday with you on your scavenger hunt."

"I knew it," I shouted. "You stole the second card from us at Aunty Penny's Arcade."

"Exsssactly," the ominous figure confirmed. "And I mussst give credit where credit isss due. I would not have dissscovered the card without you. I had ssspent all day hiding in the Tycoon'sss offissse without finding out where the cardsss were. Even with the clue he provided, it wasss only by following you that I wasss able to get the sssecond card. I'm very pleasssed that you were able to find the third for yoursssselvesss."

"I was most impressed, as well," Professor Brain-Drain added as he handed around the cookie tray.

"Don't you have any potato chips?" Tadpole asked.

I thought it was sort of impolite of him, but the Professor didn't seem to care.

"I never touch them," he replied. "I feel as if they numb my mind."

We all looked at each other in astonishment. Halogen Boy, however, wasted no time in helping himself to a sugar cookie that was shaped—and frosted—to look like the Amazing Indestructo. In fact, as I glanced down at the tray, I saw they all looked like AI.

"I have an immense appreciation for intelligence," the Professor continued as he set down the tray and picked up a cookie for himself. "I'm well aware of how rare it really is in this city," he added, before biting the head off the AI cookie he was holding.

"That card was unbelievably valuable," I pointed out. "How smart was it to make more of them?"

"Yes, yes, I know," the Professor said, waving about the headless cookie. "But some things are more important than money—things such as self-respect."

I couldn't believe what I was hearing! What kind of a crook talks like that?

"Besides," he continued, "I don't need money. I

have plenty of that. I own this entire skyscraper, after all."

"So why did you have the Multiplier create all these duplicates? And how were you able to increase his power?"

"I *am* a genius," he answered matter-of-factly. "I've been working on a device for quite some time that would enhance the power of anyone who used it. I gave a small handheld prototype of it to the Multiplier as a test—which just goes to show that even geniuses can make mistakes."

"He's not very bright," Halogen Boy added. "Did you drain his brain?"

"Well, truth be told, there really wasn't much there to drain," said the Professor with a grandfatherly laugh. "But I did take what little I could."

"And then you gave him that idiotic idea about the traffic cones?" Tadpole asked.

"Yes, I suggested it to him almost a decade ago. I figured it would keep him busy in a harmless sort of way until I had a use for him."

"And then the card situation came up," Plasma Girl concluded.

"Exactly." Brain-Drain beamed. "You kids really are quite smart."

With that, the Professor calmly clapped his hands

twice. I jumped up immediately, but I felt a hand push me back down in my chair, I tried to scream a warning to my teammates, but another hand had covered my mouth.

Thanks to the Sneak, I couldn't move or speak, but I could see everything as the motionless figures that we had thought were statues suddenly came to life and went after Hal, Tadpole, and Plasma Girl. I expected them to use their powers, but they were each easily subdued by the silent, hulking figures. From the strained looks on their faces, I could tell that both Plasma Girl and Halogen Boy were trying, but nothing was happening. Tadpole was sticking out his tongue, but it wasn't extending more than a few inches. The Professor Brain-Drain statue he had poked in the stomach a moment earlier had gone straight for him, clearly looking for a little payback. That's when I noticed that Tadpole's attacker had a mole on his nose, exactly like the last actor I had seen play the Professor on TV.

"I hope you enjoyed your lemonade. It's a recipe of my own invention and has the wonderful side effect of briefly nullifying your powers. It's a shame that you'll be losing your intelligence so soon as well," Professor Brain-Drain continued in the friendliest tone, "but I promise you, I'll make much better use of it than you ever could have."

CHAPTER TWENTY-SIX

A Collectible Catastrophe

"Let me take this opportunity to introduce you to my latest invention," Professor Brain-Drain commented pleasantly, as he indicated the animated figures that had just taken us captive. "I call them my Deadly Dumbots. It's not an entirely accurate name since they're neither robots nor completely dumb. But I liked the name—and they *can* be deadly."

"You mean they're not statues?" Halogen Boy asked.

"No. I'm afraid that was a little fib," confessed Professor Brain-Drain. "My sculpture period ended over a decade ago. These days I'm more into mobiles."

I watched Tadpole, Hal, and Plasma Girl struggle against the mindless-looking Dumbots. Without their powers, my teammates were helpless. I was being restrained by the Sneak. His hands and arms kept changing to look like either my shirt or my skin, depending on which part of me he was holding. It was pretty creepy.

"You see," the Professor continued, "these individuals all made the same mistake. They assumed that they were qualified to play me on that infernal television show. Unfortunately for them, they were wrong."

Walking from one brain-dead Brain-Drain to another, the Professor rattled off a list of their flaws.

"This one's voice was too high-pitched," he said, "while this one's ears were much too big."

In my opinion they looked the same size as the Professor's.

"This one is too short. And this one actually has hair," the Professor said with outrage as he lifted up the Deadly Dumbot's colander to reveal a full, bushy head. "And as for this one, I didn't like the way he pronounced the word *nuclear*."

Imagine what his reaction would be to a female Brain-Drain!

"But as you know," he continued, "my power is the ability to drain the intelligence of others for my own use. These just happen to be some of those whose intelligence I've drained. As I expend brain energy on my projects, it runs low, so I need to constantly replenish it."

"You've got a whole skyscraper full of victims right

here!" I pointed out. "Why take it out on us?"

"Oh, come now," he replied in surprise. "The villains in this building are my tenants. It's not good business to drain the intelligence from people who lease space from you. How will they come up with the money to pay their rent if I drain their brains? Not to mention most villains know that renting space from me comes with the added benefit of keeping their intelligence, so I always have plenty of renters."

I had to admit he made a lot of sense. But that didn't make me feel better as we were strapped into the chairs that surrounded the huge barber pole device in the center of the room. Once we were fully restrained, the Sneak and the Professor's army of Deadly Dumbots stepped back from us.

"Even as I speak," Professor Brain-Drain said, "the Multiplier is above us in my blimp hangar, making duplicates of my card—albeit at an excruciatingly slow pace. I need to recharge a new version of the device I invented that can amplify anyone's power. I call it an Oomphlifier. Like me, it's a device that runs on brain power."

"And just where did the brainpower come from to operate the device?" I asked pointedly. "The Multiplier isn't smart enough to generate it himself."

"Excellent question," Brain-Drain replied. "The

original handheld device was fully charged by me before it was given to the Multiplier. If he had used his Oomphlified powers carefully, he would have gotten a month's use out of the device. Instead, he squandered it all at once in a pointless attention-getting stunt that not only destroyed the device but also landed him in jail."

"He said you gave it to him specifically to make duplicates of the card."

"He is correct. I found out last Friday that there would be only three cards bearing my image and I was outraged. I called the Multiplier away from his traffic cone project and had him come here to try out the Oomphlifier. My mistake was in letting him take it along when I sent him to the Mighty Mart to buy up all the card packs he could find."

"That's a pretty expensive, and poorly thought-out, way to find a card," I said, intentionally trying to annoy him.

"Yes, it would have been." He frowned for the first time since we met him. "However, after the Multiplier's blunder, I came up with the same idea as you, my little friend."

"I try to choose my friends more carefully," I shot back.

"So I see." He gave my helpless teammates a sinister smile. "But, as I was saying, we did both think alike in

THE OOMPHLIFIER

A secret device invented by Professor Brain-Drain, the Oomphlifier magnifies its possessor's power by nearly a million times. In order to do this, it must be fully charged with pure brainpower, making it impractical for most citizens of Superopolis.

this case. I sent the Sneak over to Indestructo Industries to see if he could pinpoint more precisely where the three cards were. The rest of the story you know."

"Except your reason for making the duplicates in the first place," I said.

"Oh, haven't I told you?" He laughed softly to himself. "I can explain that at the same time I tell you about this machine you're all strapped to."

He stepped over to where Tadpole was trapped and lowered the dome onto his head. As he pressed a button on it, the needle of the gauge set into the metal helmet rose to its midway point.

"You see, I have created a new Oomphlifier," he explained as he removed a small, handheld device from the pocket of his lab coat.

"It already has a small charge of brainpower in it, but I need to give it a super charging. That's where this amazing machine comes in." He tapped the gauge on Tadpole's dome. "One of the many things it can do is measure the intelligence of anyone strapped to it. In this case it indicates that your friend here is of average intelligence—not bad but nothing special."

Tadpole shot the Professor an insulted glare, but he had already moved on to Plasma Girl.

"I call it the Brain Capacitor. In a way, it's a mechanical version of my own power. This device will sap an individual's intelligence and then store it for other purposes—purposes such as charging the Oomphlifier, for example. And once it's fully charged, I will give it to the Multiplier so that he can produce cards for me at an exponential rate."

"I overheard the Sneak saying that you were going to create millions of them," I accused.

"Did he say millions?" Brain-Drain asked. He lowered the dome over Plasma Girl's head. "I'm planning on making *billions*!"

"But why?"

"Why?" he said calmly as he pressed the button to turn on the indicator gauge. "Because Superopolis should know that I'm not someone to be overlooked. For nearly a decade, I have remained quietly in the background, allowing the city's image of me to be formed solely by that cretinous Amazing Indestructo. For a while, it was fine. I had my inventions and my artistic pursuits."

"That doesn't sound very villainous," I responded.

"Oh, don't be so certain." His mouth turned up in a sinister smile. "A good evil plan can be very inventive and artistic."

This guy was seriously creepy, I decided.

"But frankly," he continued, "I dropped out of the spotlight because I was bored. Plotting against the half-witted denizens of Superopolis is hardly a challenge. Then these cards were issued. AI had the audacity to release millions of them into the market, but relegated me to a mere three. Even a recluse doesn't like to be ignored, so I decided to make sure that I'm not taken for granted. Besides, now is a perfect time for the good citizens of Superopolis to become reacquainted with me, since other long-term plans will soon be coming to fruition."

I was incredibly curious as to what he meant by "long-term plans," but then he paused to inspect the arrow on Plasma Girl's helmet. I heard him make an approving noise.

"This one is quite a bit above average. That's very good!"

"What about the cards?" I insisted.

"Oh, yes, the cards," he replied as he moved on to Halogen Boy. Hal watched nervously as the dome was lowered over his head. "I'll produce as many as I need—maybe even trillions of them! And then I will drop them all over Superopolis. The first ones will simply clog the streets. Then they'll fill up the sewers. Next they'll spill out into the ocean. And then I'll drop even more. They'll start piling up like snowflakes in a blizzard. There will be mountains of them and—

"Well, this is a disappointment," Professor Brain-Drain grumbled as he examined the needle on Halogen Boy's indicator gauge. "This one isn't going to be any use at all. Well, no matter, where was I . . . ?"

"Mountains of them," Halogen Boy prompted him, apparently unaware that he had just been insulted.

"Oh, yes. There will be mountains of cards until the very life of Superopolis is choked off by them. And the last thing everyone sees as they suffocate will be my face looking back at them."

"You're insane," I cried.

"Now that's a bit unfair," Professor Brain-Drain complained. "After all, I couldn't do it without your help."

"What do you mean?" I demanded. I was pretty sure I knew exactly what he meant but I hoped I was wrong.

"Isn't it obvious?" he said as he lowered the dome onto my head. "The energy for charging the Oomphlifier, and thus duplicating the cards, is going to be drained directly from the brains of you four kids."

CHAPTER TWENTY-SEVEN

A New Deal

I looked up with horror as the brain-draining metal dome was lowered onto my head. Once the Professor had my noggin in his diabolical helmet there would be nothing stopping him from turning on his machine, draining the intelligence from all four of us, and transferring it to the Oomphlifier, which the Multiplier would then use to make trillions of collector cards under which he would drown all Superopolis—all the while leaving me and my teammates as brainless Dumbots.

Luckily, just then, the doorbell rang.

"Great nattering neurons," the Professor muttered as he halted with the helmet only an inch from my head. "Who is it now? Well, I do have an extra seat available."

He headed toward the door, leaving the Oomphlifier

sitting on a table across from us.

"Maybe it's Stench with help," said Halogen Boy.

"Why would heroes coming to our rescue ring the doorbell?" Tadpole asked. He had a point.

"All I know is that we have to get out of here," Plasma Girl whispered with a shudder. "We don't want to end up like *them*."

We looked around at the half dozen Deadly Dumbots who were once again looking more like statues than brain-drained actors. They were arranged about us in a semicircle, and it was clear that even if we could get out of our restraints, they would capture us again in an instant.

"Do any of you feel your powers returning?" I asked hopefully.

"Let me give it a shot," Plasma Girl said. But the best she could do was transform herself into a mildly jiggling gelatin.

"And I can only thtreth my tongue about thikth inthes," Tadpole confirmed as he stuck his tongue out about six inches.

"How about you, Hal?" I stretched to turn my head slightly to my right where he was strapped next to me.

In reply he began to glow fairly brightly. "I'm sorry, O Boy. This is the best I can do without being able to get to my apple juice."

It was more intense than the lighting in the laboratory but not bright enough to really do us any good. So how was I going to get us out of this mess? Of course I felt responsible. After all, I was the one who convinced my friends to come here. So it was up to me to come up with a plan to save them. Unfortunately, I was only beginning to get a germ of an idea when Professor Brain-Drain returned with his guest. I couldn't believe who it was.

"What's he doing here?" I hollered with undisguised hostility.

"That's right," said the Professor, "you already know the Tycoon, don't you?"

Sure enough, the president of Indestructo Industries was standing right here in the secret hideout of the Amazing Indestructo's most deadly foe.

"Hey, kids! Good to see you again." He waved, oblivious, or indifferent, to the fact that we were strapped down like prisoners. "Did my clue help you track down one of the three cards?"

"Yes," I replied. "It's one of the reasons we're trapped here now."

"That's too bad," he lied. "But I've got to thank you for getting the word out and letting your friends see the actual card. I hear from stores all over Superopolis that the card packs have been flying off

PROFESSOR BRAIN-DRAIN SHOWER CAPS

This shoddy item marked a low point in the history of Indestructo Industries. The first flammable version caught on like wildfire, but not in a good way. Following the recall, a second flameproof version was produced with even poorer results. The fact that most people do not have steel colanders on their heads that need protection while showering could perhaps explain this lack of demand. There was also the problem of putting something on your head which has the Brain-Drain name on it. In fact, those few consumers who actually bought one definitely felt dumber having done so.

the shelves since yesterday afternoon. And that's not all—"

"You creep," I interrupted him. "I'll never buy anything made by Indestructo Industries ever again."

I knew it sounded feeble the second I said it, but I didn't know what else to say.

"You won't have the chance, son," the Professor replied. "Your brain will soon be drained. Although, in fact, that *would* make you an ideal consumer," he added. "Anyway, what were you about to say, Tycoon?"

"I was going to mention," he continued, "that the few Professor Brain-Drain products we've created over the years have also completely sold out. There wasn't much to begin with, I admit, but it's all gone. We even finally got rid of those Professor Brain-Drain shower caps that we put out over four years ago."

"I use mine daily," the Professor responded indignantly. "And I've always argued that you don't produce nearly enough products bearing my image."

"That's why I'm here," said the Tycoon.

"Go on," said the Professor, clearly interested. He guided the Tycoon over to the table at which he had so recently hosted us. "I'm curious to hear what you're thinking. If I like it, you just might be able to go on thinking."

That made the Tycoon do a double take! I know it was kind of a mean thought, but the Tycoon drained of his intelligence might not be such a bad thing. It probably wouldn't change his power, though, and he'd still be able to make money even as a Dumbot.

"Kids have gone crazy for Professor Brain-Drain," he revealed. "They can't get enough of you! So I'm here to propose the creation of a whole new line of Professor Brain-Drain merchandise."

Clearly, the Tycoon was unaware that Professor Brain-Drain's popularity with kids was plummeting as fast as the price of his collector card. Since it had only just happened in the last few hours, there was no way the Tycoon could know—yet! Well, I wasn't going to be the one to tell him.

"Just let me show you the plans we've made," he continued, removing some large, folded sheets of paper from his briefcase. "Here, for example, is the Professor Brain-Drain Lair of Evil play set."

"It looks like an underground cavern," commented the Professor.

"No kid wants a play set that looks like a floor in an office high-rise," the Tycoon informed him.

"I see," said the Professor. "And what is this?"

"These are sketches of the Brain-Drain Power

Bike. It can go up to seventy-five miles an hour."

"But I travel by blimp," he informed the Tycoon.

"Blimps aren't big with kids. Work with me."

"What is this ropelike item?" asked the Professor. "Is it a noose?"

"Even better! You'll love this!" gushed the Tycoon. "It's the Brain-Drain Bungee Cord. Kids hook them on their ears and then wrap them around their heads to hold their brains in—like this!"

"I believe their skulls perform that function," replied Professor Brain-Drain. "What about my own line of Bunsen burners? Children still love Bunsen burners, don't they?"

"I'll check with my market research department." The Tycoon sighed in exasperation. "In the meantime, all I need is your signature on these contracts to get started."

"Ah yes, the contracts." The Professor's eyes seemed to zero in like arrows on the oily businessman. "That reminds me. This seems like the perfect time to renegotiate our earlier licensing arrangement. The one that ends in just a few short weeks."

"What are you referring to?" asked the Tycoon, who I'm sure knew exactly what the Professor was referring to.

"The licensing arrangement that I signed ten years ago that allows you to use my image in all your Amazing Indestructo TV shows, comic books, and other paraphernalia. The vast sums of money that the Amazing Indestructo has earned during this period have not gone unnoticed by me—especially as my own, once significant royalty checks have dwindled to practically nothing in recent months."

"It was a fair deal," protested the Tycoon, beginning to sweat even more. "And we still pay you what your contract requires. If your royalties are shrinking, it's only because your likeness is being used less. But that's not my fault. In fact, I'm here right now to try and do more with you, not less."

Professor Brain-Drain didn't say a word. His glasses stayed focused on the business executive.

"B-B-but if you are unhappy about it," the Tycoon stuttered nervously, "the person to complain to is AI himself. Nothing is done without his approval."

My eyes went wide with shock. What the Tycoon said couldn't be true. The Amazing Indestructo would never have made a deal with his deadliest enemy.

"You're lying!!" I yelled. "The Amazing Indestructo would never agree to that!"

It would have been better if they had said something. Instead they just looked at me and began chuckling. Now, more than ever, I knew we had to escape—if for no other reason than to warn AI about what was happening behind his back. An idea finally came together in my mind. But before I could put it into action, there was a loud roar, and suddenly something came crashing through one of the walls.

Smoke and dust billowed everywhere throughout Brain-Drain's laboratory, and both the Professor and the Tycoon rose from their seats in surprise. As the dust cleared, we all realized who had burst in.

It was the Amazing Indestructo himself. Justice was about to be served.

CHAPTER TWENTY-EIGHT
Acting the Part

"AI! Help us!" we all cried.

Our hero had come to save us at last!

AI turned and looked at us blankly, as if kids in trouble were the last thing he had expected to find here.

"In a minute, youngsters," he said. "I've got business to settle first."

And then he turned away from us. My heart sank.

"There you are, you dastardly villain," the Amazing Indestructo intoned. My heart rose again.

The Professor was standing with the Tycoon looking over marketing plans for Brain-Drain Brain Puffs Cereal—grayish puffs of corn shaped like miniature brains and fortified with two vitamins and oodles of sugar. To my surprise, though, AI strode forward, grabbed the Tycoon by the lapels of his jacket, and hoisted him into the air. He didn't pay any attention at all to Professor Brain-Drain.

That's okay, I convinced myself. He was just handling them one villain at a time.

"I was told I would find you here," AI said, clearly annoyed. "What do you have to say for yourself?"

"What are you talking about?" protested the Tycoon. "I'm here on official company business. There's an opportunity to make scads of money."

"Money isn't everything," announced the Amazing Indestructo. "You know there are areas that are off-limits."

I knew it! How could I have doubted my hero? He obviously hadn't known the awful things that the Tycoon was doing, and now he was here to fix everything.

"Forget why I came here," sputtered the Tycoon. "It's no big deal."

"What do you mean it's no big deal?" hissed the Professor. "It's a very big deal indeed."

"Look, I only set a few limits on what you can do," said the Amazing Indestructo. "If you stay within those boundaries, you can do whatever you want—as long as it sells."

My emotions were being played like a yo-yo. I

couldn't believe the cynical dealings that were behind my favorite toys, TV shows, and snack products—not to mention my one-time hero. There! I finally admitted it to myself. That was it. The Amazing Indestructo wasn't my hero anymore. He didn't deserve to be.

"The reason I'm here," AI continued, "is that you ignored one of those rules. I'm here because of that card you put into the collector packs."

"The Professor Brain-Drain card?" said the Tycoon, confused. "I only made three of them, just like you told me to."

"So it *was* you." Professor Brain-Drain glared at my former favorite superhero.

"Not the Brain-Drain card, you idiot," spat AI in an undignified manner. "I'm talking about the card for Meteor Boy."

The Tycoon visibly gulped. The corners of Professor Brain-Drain's mouth turned up slightly in an evil-looking smirk.

"I couldn't think of anybody else," the Tycoon tried to explain. "And we only made ten of them!"

"You know the rule. No references to Meteor Boy, ever," said AI.

"Ah, yes." The Professor cackled (and I do mean cackled—this was no chuckle). "Poor Meteor Boy. Any mention of him and his ill-fated first adventure brings it all back, doesn't it, my old friend? You may be invulnerable to everything, but you can't shake the guilt that you still feel for that poor lad's demise. You have tried to make him disappear from the public's collective memory, yet he still lingers in yours like a specter of shame."

The heroic expression on AI's face suddenly began to quiver, and then it dropped as fast as my opinion of him.

"*You're* the one responsible for what happened to him, not me!" accused AI as he dropped the Tycoon on the floor in a heap and turned on Professor Brain-Drain.

"Am I really?" the Professor responded, his blank glasses boring into AI's rapidly blinking eyes. "Why was Meteor Boy even there that day?"

I expected the Amazing Indestructo to let loose with his patented uppercut and knock the Professor unconscious. Instead, AI fell to his knees and started sobbing.

"Ah, yes," Professor Brain-Drain continued as he walked up to the slumped figure and laid his hand gently on his shoulder. "You call me the villain. But I never did anything so foolish as expose a youthful sidekick to such danger."

"What about us?" I hollered from where we still sat, trapped in the brain-draining device. "I'd call this 'exposing kids to danger.'"

But none of them were paying any attention to me. AI had his head in his hands. Who knew he was such a baby?

"You're right!" he blubbered. "I'm a horrible superhero."

"That's not true," the Tycoon spoke up. "You bring goodness and joy to millions."

"That's right," AI said, suddenly brightening as he lifted his face from his hands. "I am the representation of all that's good and right." And then, as if he hadn't just suffered an emotional breakdown, he stood up proudly and spoke out in his smooth-as-silk voice. "After all, I *am* the Amazing Indestructo."

What was with this guy? Now he seemed totally back to normal. Then Professor Brain-Drain spoke up again.

"Yet you surround yourself with inferior heroes to make yourself look better," tsk-tsked the Professor.

"You claim to fight a crusade against evil, but you make licensing arrangements with your vilest enemies.

And you manipulate those who adore you by selling them shoddy merchandise designed to empty their pockets and line your own. You disgust me."

It was really getting hard to tell who was the hero and who was the villain here. Sure enough, AI's mask of invincibility vanished as quickly as it had appeared. He dropped his face back into his hands and began sobbing.

"It's true," he howled. "I don't know why I feel the need to lower others in order to raise myself. I'm a dreadful person!"

I didn't know a whole lot about psychology, but I knew a major superiority-inferiority complex when I saw one. And clearly Professor Brain-Drain knew how to play AI as easily as a kazoo.

I decided it was time to put my own escape plan into action. I turned my attention to the Deadly Dumbot directly in front of me. It was the Brain-Drain actor with the mole on his nose.

"This next scene is the most important one in the movie," I suddenly shouted at him as if I were a film director.

The Dumbot looked at me vacantly for a moment without moving. Then I noticed a faint glimmer in its eyes. It turned its head toward the Professor as if looking for guidance, but Brain-Drain was too busy scolding AI to notice. So I decided to pour it on.

"When I give the word, you'll move forward and undo the straps that are holding me. And your motivation will be—Best Actor in a Brain-Drained performance!!"

Even a mindless actor can't resist the thought of an acting award. The fact that he was operating with an empty brain made it natural for him to follow the orders of whoever appeared to be the director. And right now, there was no direction coming from Professor Brain-Drain.

"Lights! Camera! Action!" I ordered.

To my surprise—it worked! The hulking dummy lumbered forward, bent over me, and undid my restraints. As I got up from my seat, I grabbed the Oomphlifier and shoved it into Hal's hand. The Professor may have accused him of not having much brainpower, but he knew exactly what to do.

Just then, I was grabbed by the Deadly Dumbot as if I were an award statuette.

"I'd like to thank my dermatologist . . ." he started to mumble just as Halogen Boy turned on his power with every ounce of strength he had.

"Close your eyes," I shouted to Plasma Girl and Tadpole, squeezing mine shut.

Even with them clenched shut, I could tell that Halogen Boy, with the aid of the Oomphlifier, was flooding the room with a light so brilliant that it would momentarily blind anyone whose eyes were open. I felt the strong arm of the Deadly Dumbot release me as he used it to shield his eyes. Feeling my way back to the Brain Capacitor, I found the restraining belt on one of my teammates and undid it.

"Thanks, O Boy," I heard Plasma Girl say. "I knew you could do it."

I immediately shifted to the left and removed Tadpole's restraint, while Plasma Girl did the same for Hal on the right. I could tell through my clenched eyes that his light was fading. The Professor had been right about the Oomphlifier's only having a small charge at the moment. But it had been enough to help us get free. I opened my eyes and saw that the Deadly Dumbots as well as the Tycoon, the Amazing Indestructo, and Professor Brain-Drain were still temporarily blinded. But I knew they wouldn't be for long.

"Let's get out of here," I suggested. We all turned to run for the exit.

We'd only made it about a dozen feet, however, when I ran smack into the softest, mushiest belly that a person could have. As I bounced onto my butt, I looked up to see the Crimson Creampuff smiling down at me. The League of Ultimate Goodness had arrived.

CHAPTER TWENTY-NINE

LUG's in Action

At this point I had no idea who was a hero and who wasn't, so my plan was to keep running toward the exit. The Crimson Creampuff was so fat and so mushy, though, that I was having a hard time getting around him.

"Whoa there, little buddy," he said. "There's nothing to worry about. The League of Ultimate Goodness is here to defend you. And more help is on the way once Moleman figures out how to dig his way up to the seventy-fifth floor."

I noticed that Spaghetti Man had stepped in front of Hal to protect him, and Major Bummer was using his huge behind to shield Tadpole. Whistlin' Dixie was also there, down on one knee talking to Plasma Girl.

"Thar, thar, lil' darlin', what's goin' on here?" she asked in a down-home sort of way, tipping her rhinestone cowgirl hat. "'Tain't nothin' the league can't handle."

"It's the Deadly Dumbots," Plasma Girl shouted. "They're coming after us again!"

Sure enough, the momentary blindness had passed, and not only were the six Deadly Dumbots attacking, but Professor Brain-Drain was fully in control of them again.

"Well, we'll all jes see 'bout that," promised Whistlin' Dixie as she stood to face the approaching Dumbots. "Wait 'til they get a listen ta my high C."

Taking a deep breath, the so-called Siren of South Superopolis whistled out a single note—a perfectly pitched high C. Unfortunately, it wasn't high enough to effectively do anything, and the Dumbots kept coming. What I found most impressive was that Dixie kept the note going strong and steady even as she grabbed Plasma Girl and started backing toward the main entrance.

"We'll handle them," said the Crimson Creampuff as he and Spaghetti Man stepped in front of Whistlin' Dixie and Plasma Girl.

Two of the Dumbots went right for the Crimson Creampuff and began punching him. Unfazed, he merely stood there and smiled. Their fists sank deep into his flabby layers of fat. Of course, he didn't seem to be fighting back. Maybe his strategy was to just stand there getting beat up until the attackers were worn out.

Meanwhile, Spaghetti Man was shooting out ropes of spaghetti from his fingertips. They coiled themselves around one of the approaching Dumbots, slowing it down. Unfortunately, it would have taken someone with less than zero intelligence to be trapped for long by wet noodles. Sure enough, the Dumbot simply raised its arms, and the flimsy pasta tore apart and slid to the floor.

"Holy Bolognese!" shouted Spaghetti Man as he turned and fled past Tadpole and Major Bummer, leaving Hal to fend for himself.

"Don't you think you should be trying to stop at least one of those guys?" Tadpole asked the major accusingly.

"I don't know why we're even bothering," groaned Major Bummer. "We can never win without AI's help anyway."

I overheard this comment from the seriously

depressed superhero and it suddenly made me think: where *was* the Amazing Indestructo? He could stop these Deadly Dumbots in a heartbeat. I looked back, keeping myself hidden behind one of Professor Brain-Drain's pieces of equipment. Unfortunately, what I found was that AI was still down on his knees, his head lowered and sobbing.

I would have to cheer the big guy up and get him out fighting. But just as I stepped out from behind the machine, I felt two invisible arms wrap around me.

"The Sneak," I grumbled. "Let me go, you creepy chameleon."

"Sssorry, sssonny," he hissed, "the bossss hasss plansss for you."

As he hauled me back over to the Brain Capacitor, I saw that Professor Brain-Drain's Deadly Dumbots had made short work of the League of Ultimate Goodness. Spaghetti Man was wrapped up in his own strands of pasta, apparently the only person in the world who couldn't break through them. One of the Dumbots was holding Whistlin' Dixie by her rhinestone bolero jacket with one hand and Plasma Girl with the other. Major Bummer, who had basically just given up and sat down on his big behind, was being guarded by another Dumbot, while yet another held Tadpole, who at least was trying to break free. Halogen Boy was similarly ensnared. None of my friends' powers had returned enough to be of any use.

The remaining two Deadly Dumbots seemed to be using the Crimson Creampuff as a soccer ball. It was pretty pathetic.

"Well now, that wasn't very difficult, was it?" Professor Brain-Drain cackled as he stepped in front of me. "Nevertheless, this has been far more trouble than I am used to dealing with. As you can see, I've known for quite some time how to handle Superopolis's greatest hero." He gestured over toward the Amazing Indestructo. "I may be his greatest nemesis, but he's never been mine."

He silently stared at me for a few moments through those thick, blank-looking glasses. "You, however, seem to be the primary cause of today's turmoil." It was almost like I could see the gears turning in his head as he planned his next move.

"Sneak, strap him back to the Brain Capacitor," he finally spoke.

"Asss you wisssh," Sneak replied.

While the Sneak was buckling me back in, this time all by myself, Professor Brain-Drain bent over and retrieved the handheld Oomphlifier that Hal had drained and discarded only a few moments earlier. I watched him plug it into the charging device, which in turn was hooked into the Brain Capacitor itself.

"Now, let's see exactly what we have here," the Professor mused as he lowered the shiny silver dome onto my head.

This time the helmet was set in place and I heard Professor Brain-Drain switch on the measuring gauge. He gasped.

"Great gamma globulins!" he exclaimed. "This is impossible."

"What's impossible?" I shouted.

I was worried that something was wrong. Wait—I should clarify that. I was worried something was wrong *other* than the fact that an evil genius had me strapped to a machine that would soon suck out all my intelligence.

Brain-Drain paid no attention to me. Instead, he reached over to the charging device that the Oomphlifier was plugged into, and switched it on. He then reached for the Brain Capacitor's main switch and turned it on as well. I instantly felt a tingle running through my head. Exactly one second later I heard a bell go ping on the charging device.

"What's happened?" I asked with alarm, wondering if my intelligence was all gone. I shuddered at the thought that it could have taken only a second. Then I realized that the very fact I could ask myself those questions meant my intelligence was still intact. The only explanation had to be that the machine had failed somehow. Or had it? Professor Brain-Drain did not look unhappy. In fact he looked positively ecstatic as he raised his left hand and extended a long bony finger toward my skull.

Then I realized he was planning to finish the job by manually draining the rest of my brain directly into his own. But just as Professor Brain-Drain's finger was about to touch my forehead, a strange thing happened—a taxicab came flying through the hole in the wall that the Amazing Indestructo had created. As we all turned to watch, it came screeching to a halt in the middle of the Professor's lair. What was even odder was the fact that Stench was lying on top of it.

CHAPTER THIRTY
The New New Crusaders

As the Levitator stepped out of the car, it became clear how a taxicab had gotten up to the seventy-fifth floor of a skyscraper. I guessed that once Lev had raised the taxi to the proper height, Stench had used his own particular talent to propel the car through the hole in the wall. The Levitator was followed out of the cab by the Big Bouncer, Windbag, and . . .

"*Dad!*" I hollered. "He's trying to drain my brain!"

"Over my dead body," my dad growled, heading for Professor Brain-Drain, his hands already glowing bright red.

"Look out, Dad," I warned him.

Three Deadly Dumbots came right at him. One of them dove at my father and knocked him to the ground. The other two piled on a moment later. I immediately heard one of them start to scream, and I knew Dad was laying on the heat. Thankfully, additional help was also on the way.

The Big Bouncer came crashing through, knocking two of the Dumbots off my father. Next, the Levitator grabbed both Dumbots by the ankles and hoisted them harmlessly into the air where they couldn't reach any of us.

The remaining three Dumbots came running toward the new arrivals, but they ran into a solid blast of air from Windbag.

Now free, the members of the League of Ultimate Goodness rejoined the fight as well. Spaghetti Man grabbed an umbrella and used it to whack one of the Dumbots. Major Bummer sat down on the one who had been guarding him and began telling him all his troubles. Whistlin' Dixie provided an exciting background fight melody. And the Crimson Creampuff, no longer being used as a kickball, was renewing some family ties.

"BB!" he shouted at the Big Bouncer. "It's me!"

"CC?" the Big Bouncer replied. "What are you doing here, little brother?"

"I'm here to kick some bad guy butt!" he yelled. "Are you ready to help me?"

"Let's do it," BB answered.

With that, the Big Bouncer propelled himself into an oncoming Dumbot and sent him sailing right toward his younger brother. The Dumbot landed right in the center of the Crimson Creampuff's ample belly and seconds later was ricocheting into the upper recesses of Brain-Drain's lair.

"This just won't do at all," Professor Brain-Drain commented mildly as he watched his Deadly Dumbots being dispatched one by one. Retrieving the Oomphlifier and shoving it into his pocket, he turned back to me. "I believe it's time to depart. And *you* will be coming with me."

"Wait a minute!" a voice shouted to the Professor. It was the Tycoon. "Don't forget your contracts. When you've had a chance to look them over, just sign them and send them back to me."

The Professor grabbed the briefcase full of contracts in one hand. Then, quickly unlatching me from the Brain Capacitor, he grabbed me by the arm and dragged me behind him up the central circular stairway. Dad was still fighting with a pair of Dumbots and couldn't see what was happening.

"Up we go to the blimp." Professor Brain-Drain cheerily hummed to himself. "Do you enjoy blimps? Of course you do. All children love blimps."

"Let me go." I struggled. "And, no, I don't like

blimps!"—even though I sort of did.

But I couldn't break free of that skeletal grip that crazy old men always seem to have, and soon we were up on the catwalk that led to the moorings where the blimp awaited us. As we got closer, I saw the Multiplier in the gondola carriage.

"Lock the boy in the blimp," said the Professor to the Multiplier, handing over me and the briefcase full of contracts. "Then come with me."

The Multiplier did as he was told. Trapped in the blimp I watched the Professor and the Multiplier head over to a small room where I assumed the tethering mechanism was located. As they disappeared, I turned to check out the interior of the blimp. It actually looked fairly homey. In fact, it looked like an entertainment room. There was a small kitchen area, a television set, a rug, some furniture, and . . . a Ping-Pong table? Well, why not?

Maybe it was just a habit, but with nothing else to do, I instinctively walked over and turned on the TV. To my surprise, what popped onto the screen was a shot of the Professor's lair. And it was a live shot. I could see the battle going on between the Deadly Dumbots, the League of Ultimate Goodness, and my father's team (I couldn't quite bring myself to call them by their awful new name just yet).

The Multiplier and Professor Brain-Drain soon reappeared. The Professor seemed a little jittery as he stepped into the gondola, but he was calm again by the time he took the controls of the blimp and began backing it away from the spire of the Vertigo Building.

Just then I heard an explosion, and a blinding flash illuminated even the darkest nooks and crannies of the spire's interior. For a moment I thought I saw a figure in white still standing on the catwalk. *The Sneak*, I thought to myself. *He got left behind! Ha!* And then there was another burst of color. From the chords of calliope music I was hearing, my bet was that Tadpole

had gotten his hands on the Combustible Calliope and was giving it its test run.

I turned back to the screen to see if anyone would be coming to my rescue anytime soon. Things down below looked like they were just about wrapped up even amid the fireworks. Stench had grabbed the Levitator's two Dumbots right out of the air and, knocked their heads together, leaving them unconscious. Counting the one that had been put out of commission by the Crimson Creampuff and the Big Bouncer, and the two that Major Bummer and Spaghetti Man had incapacitated, only one was still causing trouble.

Dad finally got the last Dumbot off him—the Professor Brain-Drain with hair—by pressing his hands against the mindless creature's face and delivered a searing blast of heat. It ran off howling with a bright red handprint on each cheek. Then Dad was on his feet in under a second, calling out for me.

"OB!" I could hear him holler both on the screen and from a distance, even though the blimp was drifting away from the building at that point.

"I'm on the blmmmp," I tried to holler back just as the Multiplier covered my mouth with his hand.

But Dad had heard me, and I could see him standing in the gaping hole in the side of the building staring back helplessly at me. I should have known he wouldn't let that stop him though.

Desperately, he looked about the laboratory and immediately spotted the invention that Brain-Drain had called the Icarus III. Jumping aboard it he began to pedal. The wings started flapping right away and he was soon barreling toward the hole in the wall. Fortunately, the wings fell off almost immediately. If they had waited until he was out of the building it would have been bad news for Dad. On the TV, I watched him bolt over to the Levitator.

"Lev, you've gotta get me out to that blimp," he implored.

"I wish I could, Thermo," he said helplessly. "But I can only levitate things up and down. I'm not the Propellerator!"

"This guy can get you there," Windbag said huffily, pointing at the Amazing Indestructo.

I could see that AI wasn't sobbing anymore, but he still looked beaten down. Tentatively, he glanced up as all four members of the New New Crusaders stepped up to him. Okay, so I said it. But it's still a stupid name for a team.

"What about it, AI?" said the Big Bouncer. "Thermo's son is on that blimp and you're the only one who can get Thermo over to it."

"You didn't help us fight," pointed out the Levitator, "so here's your chance to make up for it."

The Amazing Indestructo looked pathetically from one to the other.

"It's no use," he wailed. "I'm a failure as a hero and as a human being."

"That may be true—" Windbag started to say, but he was interrupted.

"You fellers jes need ta know the right sorta things to say," Whistlin' Dixie said as she barged her way into the conversation. "And a course how ta say 'em."

Taking a deep breath, and pulling her spangly rodeo gloves on tight, Dixie went to work.

"Oh, you big handsome feller you." She batted her eyes. "Ah hear yer the most powerfulest hero thar ever dern was."

Sure enough, AI looked up and his eyes were no longer teary—but focused on the damsel in distress. "Yes, ma'am," he replied, still a little weakly. "That is what they say."

"Then only you can help lil' ole me," she said, pouring it on. "Will ya?"

"Of course," he said a little more firmly as he once again got to his feet.

"Ya done such a darlin' job moppin' up all these nasty criminals here." She waved her hand across the field of victory that AI had had no part in.

"Well, ma'am, that is my job." A corner of his mouth rose in a rakish smile as he surveyed the wreckage.

"Well, thar's a lil' buckaroo who still needs rescuin', and someone has to take that tyke's poor papa out thar and help him save the boy."

"A perfect job for the Amazing Indestructo," he boasted, apparently fully back to his normal superior self. "Let's go!"

Windbag and the Levitator, standing on either side of Dixie, gaped in amazement.

"They don't keep me aroun' jes fer ma whistlin'," she said, giving them a wink.

Most important, the Amazing Indestructo started up his rocket pack and grabbed my dad from behind, hooking his elbows beneath his arms. As the fires from the rocket pack built up to a roar, the two heroes blasted off toward me and the blimp.

"Let's go save your boy!"

CHAPTER THIRTY-ONE

The Price of Popularity

They were coming to rescue me! Now I just had to keep the Professor distracted until they got here . . . hopefully before he remembered to drain my brain.

Professor Brain-Drain set the blimp on autopilot, got up from the controls, and came back to find the Multiplier. I stayed carefully out of the way.

"There you are," Brain-Drain said in exasperation when he found the Multiplier sitting on the edge of the Ping-Pong table, smugly bouncing one of the balls with a paddle. "Are you ready to do your job at last?"

An evil-looking leer spread across the Multiplier's face as he withdrew the fully-charged Oomphlifier from a pocket in his costume.

"Now you'll see my power unleashed," he sneered at me.

"No," the Professor corrected him, "it's *my* power. I just happen to be lending it to you for my own purposes."

Professor Brain-Drain strolled to the back of the blimp and pulled open a hatch in the floor. A huge empty cargo area was situated below.

"Your job," the Professor continued, "is to fill this cargo bay with my collector card. It should hold about two million of them. You have ten minutes. I want to drop this first load over Lava Park."

The Multiplier removed the original card from a pocket in his costume. Touching it just briefly, he handed it over to the Professor, who slipped it into his lab coat. Then the Multiplier extended his arms, spread out the fingers of both hands . . . and concentrated. In less than a second Professor Brain-Drain cards started shooting from his hands with such speed that he looked like a magician performing the world's most spastic card trick.

"Ahhhh, ha-ha-ha-haha-ha!" He let out that incredibly annoying maniacal laugh of his. "Witness the awesome power of the— Ouch!!"

I couldn't help it. I kicked him in the back of his knee. I think he was about to turn on me, but a sharp rebuke from the Professor stopped him.

"Keep making the cards," he commanded. "I'll

take care of this one."

With that, Professor Brain-Drain dragged me toward the front of the blimp. I was sure this was it for my brain. How to distract him? I spotted the briefcase filled with the Tycoon's contracts for a whole new line of Brain-Drain products.

"No kid in Superopolis is going to want any stupid Professor Brain-Drain merchandise," I blurted out.

"You wound me, son," said Professor Brain-Drain, looking genuinely upset. "Why would you say such a hurtful thing?"

"It's true," I pressed. "And it's your own fault. Yesterday, before you started creating these duplicates, every kid I know was talking about you. You were even more popular than the Amazing Indestructo. Kids were offering to trade thirty-two AI cards for just one of yours."

"Were they really?" Brain-Drain asked, his face brightening. "I always hoped that children would someday recognize my appeal. I must admit that it's nice to be loved—even by those one is planning to destroy."

"Well, thanks to you, that love only lasted about twenty-four hours," I informed him. "As soon as you sent the Sneak around this morning to sell the Multiplier's first duplicates the situation began to change. When kids found out your card wasn't rare anymore, your popularity dropped as fast as AI's self-respect."

"But I never sent the Sneak out to sell the cards," said the Professor. "My plan was merely to destroy all Superopolis with them."

"I guess he decided on his own that there was some money to be made," I concluded. "While following me and my friends, he must have figured out what those cards could be worth and decided to make some extra money on the side."

"Sneak!!" Professor Brain-Drain hollered, looking around the blimp's control room. As I had suspected, there was no sign of him. The Sneak had snuck off.

"He probably slipped away in all the confusion before we even got on the blimp," I said. "And now your short-lived popularity has been ruined."

"Yes, that's probably true," he agreed wistfully. "But tell me again, were children really more interested in me than in the idiotic Indestructo?"

"Yes," I said, "but you'll never be able to regain their affections if you bury them under trillions of cards. And now that I think about it, why are you making licensing arrangements anyway if you're planning on destroying the entire city?"

"They're both valid forms of self-promotion," he responded, "and if one doesn't work, hopefully the other will. A true genius never puts all his potato chips in one bowl. The truth is I have several fiendish plots that have been brewing for decades. I haven't moved forward with most of them because they don't provide a challenge. As you yourself have come to realize, the Amazing Indestructo is a buffoon. Outwitting him is about as difficult as cheating at solitaire."

Then he looked directly at me, his head tilting slightly, and a shiver ran down my spine.

"Without a worthy opponent, the thrill of destruction just isn't the same."

Even as he spoke, I could tell his mind was shifting gears. And I couldn't help but get a creepy feeling that what it was shifting to was—me. I began to back away.

"Speaking of destruction," he said. He was now

looking at me the way a starving man looks at a pot roast. "As helpful as it is as a storage device, you know I don't need the Brain Capacitor in order to drain someone of their intelligence. The old-fashioned method works just fine."

Raising his left arm, he pointed his index finger at me and advanced to within an inch of my forehead.

"It almost seems a shame," he said sadly. "Given time, you might have developed into a truly interesting adversary."

As his finger came in contact with my forehead, the last thing I heard was my own sharp intake of breath. Then everything exploded.

CHAPTER THIRTY-TWO

Thermo to the Rescue

I opened my eyes and saw chaos. The Amazing Indestructo was holding Professor Brain-Drain up in the air with one arm, while an even greater superhero was rushing toward me.

"Dad!" I cried out in relief as I ran and threw my arms around him.

"Take it easy, hero," he said. "I'm here, and everything is going to be fine."

"Don't let Professor Brain-Drain say too much to AI," I warned my father. "He might turn him into a whimpering wreck again."

But apparently, the Amazing Indestructo had pulled himself together enough to finally lash back at his archenemy.

"You're in default of our agreement!" he hollered.

It wasn't exactly the heroic challenge I would have hoped for, but it seemed pretty typical for the AI I'd so recently come to know and disrespect.

"You know our contract says you cannot interfere with the production and distribution of any Indestructo Industries merchandise," AI said indignantly. He motioned toward the Multiplier at the back of the blimp. "Your unauthorized copying of these collector cards obviously violates our deal."

"Yes, a deal that ends quite soon." The Professor chuckled. "Perhaps you thought that by only manufacturing three copies of my card, you would make it seem like I was losing popularity, and thus I'd be in a weaker position to renegotiate."

From the guilty-looking expression on the Amazing Indestructo's face, I could tell that the Professor had hit it right on the head. This whole collector card crisis was just because AI wanted to be in a better position to renew a contract with Professor Brain-Drain. From the look on my dad's face, I could tell he was appalled as well.

"Maybe what you need is a new archenemy," the Professor said. "I'm sure someone like the Human Jellyfish would be available to take my place. Good luck with that! Meanwhile, I'll continue with my own plan to reestablish my fiendish reputation with the good people of Superopolis."

From the way his arm holding the Professor began to drop, I could tell that AI might actually cave in.

"You're going to bargain with him?!" I blurted out. "Even as he attempts to destroy Superopolis?"

"A hero has to have an archnemesis," AI shrugged.

"Not under contract!" my father said.

"Oh, like you understand what it takes to maintain an ongoing relationship with a name-brand supervillain," the Amazing Indestructo snapped.

"Your archenemy should be 'maintained' by the Superopolis Correctional Facility if you've done your job right!"

The Professor interrupted them. "Perhaps it might interest you all to know that we are currently dropping toward the earth at a velocity that some might consider dangerous."

We all looked out the window to see the blimp drifting less than a couple hundred feet above Superopolis's warehouse district. I guess the added weight of AI and my dad was more than the airship could handle. Then it occurred to me that if the Multiplier had done his job properly (always a very big if) there were also close to two million Professor Brain-Drain cards weighing us down. I turned to look toward the back of the car. Sure enough, he was heading right for us, his primary job completed.

"Look out, Dad," I warned. "It's the Multiplier."

"You!" screamed the Multiplier as Dad turned to face him. Apparently he suddenly remembered who had actually stopped him at the Mighty Mart. "You'll regret ever having tangled with the Multiplier!"

"I doubt it," my father replied calmly.

The Multiplier raised his hands, and I shielded my face. But I should have known that if anyone could mess up an attack it would be him. Reaching for the nearest object, which just happened to be a Ping-Pong ball, he began making more and flinging them at us. I grabbed both the paddles and tossed one to Dad. Using mine, I swatted away the balls coming at me from the Multiplier's left hand. Dad didn't even bother swinging. The balls simply bounced off him as if they were no more than drops of rain.

"Stay away from me," the Multiplier wailed as the mighty Thermo walked right up to him and smacked him over the head with the Ping-Pong paddle.

"Don't ever mess with my kid again," he snarled as the Multiplier crumpled to the floor.

Dad hadn't bothered to set the paddle on fire. He just gave the Multiplier a good old-fashioned whupping. Of course, the floor was now full of Ping-Pong balls, and we were in serious danger of slipping on them. I rushed over to the gondola's side boarding door, unlatched it, and swung it open. The balls rolled to that side of the blimp and continued right out the door.

Then I walked over to the unconscious Multiplier and picked up the Oomphlifier. I slipped it into my pocket just as he began to stir. To be honest, I felt a little sorry for the Multiplier. I mean, sure, his only goal in life was to do evil, but he was so pitiful at it I couldn't help but feel bad for him. So I decided to give him some advice.

"You know," I whispered to him, "you could start your own company selling traffic cones and make a fortune. You didn't pay anything for them, so you could sell them for less than anyone else."

"I won't need them," he hissed. "I'll just use my Oomphlifier to . . ."

He began feeling around for the missing device and I slowly backed away from him. Even as stupid as he was, he would soon figure out that I was the one who—

"Where is it?!" he shrieked. "You've stolen my power!"

In a flash, he was up on his feet, past my dad, and coming my way. Luckily, I ducked just as he lunged at me. His scream blared in my ear at first, but then trailed off dramatically. But then I guess that's natural for someone who's just dived through an open door and was now plummeting toward the ground. I ran to the doorway and looked down just in time to see him crash through the glass skylight in the roof of a building. The second before he hit, I realized that it was his very own warehouse. I heard a muffled *fump* as he landed in what I figured had to be a pile of traffic cones.

"Think about what I said!" I hollered. The blimp began to rise now that it was minus the weight of one Multiplier. Looking ahead, I saw we were once again on course for Lava Park.

Meanwhile, the discussion was continuing between the Amazing Indestructo and Professor Brain-Drain.

"If you expect me to renew our deal," the Professor insisted, "I demand a minimum guarantee, as well as my own advertising jingle."

"Please! You'll have to speak with the Tycoon." AI turned his head nobly away.

"Don't just stand there negotiating," my dad exploded. "Haul him off to jail!"

"I can't, I'm afraid," AI admitted with a resigned sigh. "Our agreement prohibits me from arresting him."

"What kind of a hero are you?!" I shouted in disbelief. "Besides, he's already broken your contract!"

"*He* may have, but I'm a hero. A hero always honors his agreements." AI held his nose up as if he had something to be proud of.

"A hero doesn't make deals with his archenemy to

begin with," I pointed out with disgust. As good as it felt to say, though, I really wished I hadn't.

"That's true," AI admitted as his eyes began to blink rapidly and his lower lip started to quiver. When his shoulders slumped, he loosened his grip on the Professor.

"Don't let go of Brain-Drain!" I cried out.

But it was too late. The Professor was free and running toward the back of the blimp. So I did the only thing I could think of—I stuck out my foot and tripped him. As he skidded onto the floor, the colander on his head went flying, and Dad charged him.

"Dad," I hollered, "take care of Brain-Drain!"

My father was obviously a lot stronger than creaky old Professor Brain-Drain, but only as long as he could keep the Professor from touching his head and draining away his intelligence. The two were soon tangled in a struggle.

"Don't let him touch your head," I shouted. "Keep his hands away from you until I can get AI to help."

It was just like AI to leave the dangerous work to my dad, while he wasted time sobbing and berating himself. It really bothered me to think about how misguided my hero worship had been. But I saw we were almost to Lava Park, and the Professor would be desperate to release the two million cards stashed in the hold. So I

swallowed my pride and did what I had to do.

"Aren't you the Amazing Indestructo?" I said with as much awe as I could stomach.

I stepped over to him and placed my hand on his shoulder.

"I am," he answered a little bit hesitantly.

"All this time, Superopolis's greatest hero has been right in front of my eyes," I said, but I was no longer

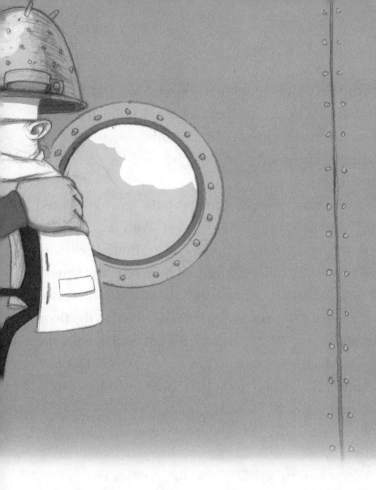

looking at AI. Instead, I spoke directly to my father. "And I only just realized it."

Dad understood me and a proud smile spread across his face.

"It's such an honor," I said turning back to an oblivious AI. And then I poured it on. "It must be hard to be so perfect."

"Well, it isn't easy," he admitted.

"If there's anyone who can rescue me and my dad from that evil Professor Brain-Drain, I know it's you." I gave him my wide-eyed, innocent look, topped off with my best worried pout.

It worked.

The Amazing Indestructo got to his feet and started toward the two struggling figures. With a surprising amount of force for a skinny old man, Professor Brain-Drain unleashed a solid kick right against my father's shin. My dad let out a howl and dropped the Professor, who ran toward the cargo door lever. Dad fell to the floor, his hands hitting the rug to catch his fall. Still in pain, the heat in his hands soared and the rug erupted in flames.

"Quick, AI," I hollered, "get rid of the rug before it causes any damage!"

"But it's on fire," he said, looking at me like I was nuts.

"You're indestructible!!" I yelled back at him.

"Okay, okay," he said, "there's no need to get huffy."

Then, as the fire spread across the entire rug, the Amazing Indestructo grabbed hold of it by a corner and did possibly the stupidest thing he could have done. Instead of pushing it out the open door, he dragged it over to the hold. With one kick, he sent it tumbling into the midst of two million Professor Brain-Drain cards.

"So much for those contract violations," he said

proudly. The cards, of course, caught fire instantly. It was only a matter of seconds before the flames whipped up into the gondola.

"We have to get out of here," I shouted to AI, who seemed surprised that millions of bits of cardboard would react to fire that way. "You'll have to carry both of us."

Dad was just getting to his feet, but I could tell he was still in pain.

"Get up on my shoulders," AI instructed me, and I wasted no time in following his directions.

Then, once again, the Amazing Indestructo got behind my father and slipped his elbows beneath his arms. AI fired his rockets and we shot out of the flaming blimp. I looked back and saw that it was headed straight for Mount Reliable in the center of Lava Park. As it drifted over the volcano's mouth, lava erupted into the air, engulfing what remained of the blimp. It was precisely five o'clock.

CHAPTER THIRTY-THREE

After Math

I showed up at school the next morning with a note from Mom and Dad for Miss Marble. It said:

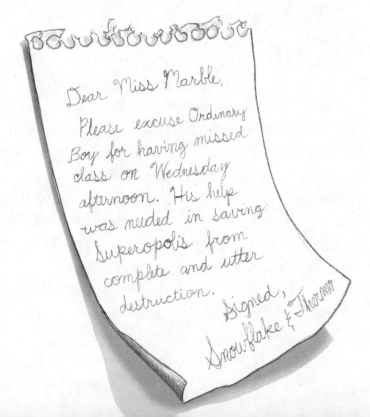

Dear Miss Marble,

Please excuse Ordinary Boy for having missed class on Wednesday afternoon. His help was needed in saving Superopolis from complete and utter destruction.

Signed,
Snowflake & Thermo

Stench, Plasma Girl, and Tadpole were already there. They had brought notes from their parents as well. In addition, Plasma Girl had brought along that morning's edition of *The Superopolis Times*. I read the headline aloud.

"AI Pulls Plug on Brain-Drain," I announced. "Professor Probably Perishes," it said in smaller type below. The picture is what really caught my eye, though. It was a shot of the Amazing Indestructo arriving back at the Vertigo Building carrying my dad, and with me riding on his shoulders.

"Hey, that's the picture Whistlin' Dixie snapped as we returned," I pointed out.

"Wait until you read the caption." Plasma Girl smirked.

"'AI saves unnamed father and son from fiery death,'" I repeated. "Yeah, that he nearly caused! Boy, you can't believe anything you read in the papers."

"Check out what's below the fold," Tadpole said.

I flipped the paper around to find another photo. This one was of the members of the League of Ultimate Goodness who also participated in the fight. Except it wasn't just them. I could clearly see Windbag and the Levitator standing with them. I read the picture caption aloud.

"'The League of Ultimate Goodness participates

in AI's incredible victory, along with members of an unknown group.' Can you believe this?"

"Hey, my dad thought it was great," Stench spoke up. "He said most groups would kill for that kind of PR their first time out. Besides, have you heard what they're calling themselves? I actually think 'unknown group' has a better ring to it."

"Well, if you ask me," I said, "the group that proved themselves the most was a team called the Junior Leaguers."

"You know it," Tadpole agreed excitedly. "We took on Professor Brain-Drain, the evilest bad guy of them all, and we brought him down!"

"Well, not completely on our own," Plasma Girl interjected. "There were about a dozen other heroes that helped."

"None of whom would have been there if we hadn't led the way," Tadpole argued back, as usual.

"Stop quarreling," Stench said. "We never would have gone there at all if O Boy hadn't convinced us to act like heroes."

Stench was right. But the truth was, I felt guilty about leading my team into such a dangerous situation. I was just relieved that it had all turned out okay.

"We did behave like heroes," Plasma Girl agreed. "Three cheers for the Junior Leaguers!"

Just then the school bus pulled up in front of us. As soon as the door opened, Halogen Boy came running out, pursued by a group of our fellow classmates.

"I'll thell you my Profethor Brain-Drain card for one thiny dime," I heard Melonhead sputtering, seeds splattering against the back of Hal's head as he tried to get away.

"Me, too," hollered Transparent Girl. "And mine is nicer than Melonhead's."

"Buy mine," insisted Lobster Boy. "Dad told me that if I wanted a new bike, I'd have to buy it myself—and I need the money!"

"I'll sell you all three of mine for a dime," volunteered Puddle Boy.

"But I've already got one," Hal protested, flashing them the card he had bought from the Banshee the day before. He ducked behind us in an attempt to hide from the frantic mob.

"Don't they know that all the other Professor Brain-Drain cards have been destroyed?" Stench muttered as Halogen Boy took shelter behind him.

That made me realize something.

"Don't hide from all these eager sellers," I told Hal. "We want to buy up every card we can."

"Why?" asked Tadpole.

"Just trust me," I said. "Hal, it's time to start buying."

Melonhead caught up with him right at that moment, waving his Professor Brain-Drain card wildly in the air.

"Jutht a thingle tholitary dime," he insisted.

Halogen Boy hesitantly slipped his hand into his pocket, held it there for a second, and then slowly retrieved a single dime.

"You're getting yourthelf a thteal," said Melonhead as he grabbed the dime from Hal's hand and shoved the card at him. It was sticky with watermelon juice.

Everyone else elbowed their way closer as, one by one, Hal exchanged dimes for Professor Brain-Drain cards. At lunchtime word had spread among the other classes, and by the time school was over we had managed to purchase every one of the remaining duplicate Brain-Drain cards.

As we walked to team headquarters after school, I shuffled through the cards. There were about seventy-five of them altogether. Some had mold on them, some were clawed up, some were in collector bags, and one of them even looked like it had been deep fried. But the important thing was that they all belonged to us.

When we got to Stench's place his dad was working in the backyard. He'd obviously just finished using his power to blow all the leaves into one big pile. Now he was burning them a few armfuls at a time in a big metal barrel. I walked up to it and asked Windbag if he would mind me getting rid of some garbage.

"Go right ahead, O Boy," he replied, "I'm just getting the yard cleaned up in case anyone from the press wants to come by and interview me."

Clearing the leaves really didn't do a whole lot to make a junkyard look nicer, but I didn't say anything. Instead, I strolled over to the flaming barrel.

"What are you doing?" Tadpole yelled as I took the stack of phony cards and dropped them into the fire.

"He must know what he's doing," Plasma Girl said, holding him back, "unless Professor Brain-Drain sapped some of his smarts."

I ignored the comment as I turned and began climbing up the ladder to our headquarters.

"Is that what happened?" Tadpole pressed as they followed me. "You seemed fine up until Brain-Drain kidnapped you."

"It's true," I said, smiling to myself. "But you weren't there when he started draining away my intelligence on his blimp. If AI and my dad had arrived any later, who knows how much I would have left?"

"Wow," said Stench, "that must have been pretty scary. Do you feel like you're dumber?"

"Sure he is," said Tadpole as he plopped down on the couch. "Why else would he have just burned all those cards we spent the entire day buying?"

"It doesn't make very much sense," Halogen Boy agreed.

"Yeah, I guess you're right," I said, glancing over to our Hall of Trophies and the one, the only, remaining Professor Brain-Drain card left in existence. "It doesn't make any sense at all."

PROFESSOR BRAIN-DRAIN

Ordinary Boy returns for
more extraordinary adventures in

THE EXTRAORDINARY ADVENTURES OF

ORDINARY BOY

BOOK TWO
THE RETURN
OF METEOR BOY?

Years ago, a young hero named Meteor Boy mysteriously disappeared during a dangerous mission. Now Ordinary Boy is determined to uncover the truth once and for all. What really happened during that final battle? What secrets are the original members of the League of Ultimate Goodness hiding? And the biggest question of all . . . who was Meteor Boy?